After Dinner Conversation

This magazine publishes fi_____ philosophical questions in an info_____ _____ _____ is to generate thoughtful discussion in an open and easily accessible manner.

Names, characters, businesses, organizations, places, events, and incidents are either the product of the author's imagination or are used fictitiously. Any resemblance to actual persons, living or dead, events, or locales is entirely coincidental. The magazine is published monthly in print and electronic format.

All rights reserved. After Dinner Conversation Magazine is published by After Dinner Conversation, Inc., a 501(c)(3) nonprofit in the United States of America. No part of this magazine may be used or reproduced in any manner without written permission from the publisher. Abstracts and brief quotations may be used without permission for citations, critical articles, or reviews. Contact the publisher at info@afterdinnerconversation.com.

ISSN# 2693-8359   Vol. 4, No. 4

Copyright © 2023 After Dinner Conversation
Editor in Chief: *Kolby Granville*
Story Editor: *R.K.H. Ndong*
Acquisitions Editor: *Stephen Repsys*
Cover Design: *Shawn Winchester*
Design, layout, and discussion questions by After Dinner Conversation.

https://www.afterdinnerconversation.com

After Dinner Conversation believes humanity is improved by ethics and morals grounded in philosophical truth and that philosophical truth is discovered through intentional reflection and respectful debate. In order to facilitate that process, we have created a growing series of short stories across genres, a monthly magazine, and two podcasts. These accessible examples of abstract ethical and philosophical ideas are intended to draw out deeper discussions with friends, family, and students.

Table Of Contents

FROM THE EDITOR .... - 3 -

THORN .... - 5 -

WHAT WE TALK ABOUT WHEN WE TALK ABOUT REINCARNATION .... - 24 -

THE HOUSE OF GOD .... - 43 -

VISIONS OF MIDWIVES .... - 51 -

PLAYING GOD .... - 64 -

AND JOY SHALL OVERTAKE US AS A FLOOD .... - 80 -

BOOMCHEE .... - 108 -

AUTHOR INFORMATION .... - 120 -

ADDITIONAL INFORMATION .... - 122 -

* * *

From the Editor

I'm not going to lie, there is a lot of God in this issue. This isn't a God-themed issue. It just randomly worked out that way based on the order of our submissions. Last year we had an issue that was almost entirely about punishment and prison sentences. I can only hope that someday we will have an issue that focuses on cowboys and circus animals...

However, proofreading this issue does make me wonder why God (*either a belief or lack of belief*) features so prevalently in questions about ethics, values, and right-decision making. I am in no way qualified to opine on this topic, and I'm apt to think anything I say will be both myopic and simplistic, with a touch of "there, there, look, the town fool tries so hard..." So, hard pass on discussing that topic...

What I can say is this magazine—and our mission to encourage thoughtful discussions among the citizenry about right societal values—is part of a human timeline-spanning continuum. The very process of reading this magazine means you, too, are part of that noble continuum. And there is honor in that. As always, there is honor in the effort.

I should also mention, we finally have a professional cover design artist. I hope you enjoy the new covers moving forward. Be sure to tell the cowboys and circus animals.

Kolby Granville – Editor

Thorn

Erik Fatemi

* * *

Joseph was never anyone I had to worry about. Joseph was a nobody. He did his work, went home to his family. That's as far as his ambitions went. If you needed someone to build a door, fix a stone wall—odd jobs like that—and you didn't have much money, you hired Joseph. He had his regulars, but not enough to cut into my business. Most of the time, verily, I forgot he even existed. So, no, Joseph wasn't my problem. My problem was his boy. I just didn't see it coming.

The first sign came about ten years ago. I was walking through the market, and, lo, there was Philip, the son of Matthias, in his usual stall, chattering nonstop to everyone who passed by. The finest pottery in town! The lowest prices! But I wasn't interested in his bowls and platters. My eyes went straight to two new cedar stools that he'd set out for customers. The seats, rectangular and contoured, were unlike any I'd seen before in Sepphoris. I'd already taken over most of the labor in town, and none of my people were capable of such craftsmanship. This was Temple-quality work. Whoever built these stools wouldn't be selling to potters for long. He'd go where the money was, to a better clientele. My clientele. I'd seen it before. In fact, I'd done the same thing myself when I was breaking into the business.

I needed to find out who made these stools.

Philip fussed over me when he saw me coming, and I took a seat. I'm tall, nearly four cubits, and I eat well. Most stools would prefer a lighter load, but this one supported me easily. I picked up an oil lamp from among his wares and pretended to examine it.

"Martha will love it," Philip said. He listed its many virtues in great detail and quoted a price we both knew was too high. He also knew I'd pay it, because I could.

I considered the offer, then rapped my knuckles on the empty stool next to me. "Not bad. Where'd you get them?"

Philip stammered, nervous he was about to lose a sale. "You know I always buy from you, Timothy. But—"

I smiled and held up my hand. "Just curious."

When he said Joseph, the son of Jacob, I made him repeat it. Impossible. Where did Joseph learn how to make stools like this?

* * *

James arrived at my house early the next morning, as usual, to review my affairs for the day. Sepphoris was booming, and it was a good time to be in construction. I'd known James since school, but we were never what you'd call friends. Other boys mocked him and called him James the Lesser because he was the smallest of the three Jameses in our class and as meek as a lamb. But I tolerated him. He followed me around, hanging on my every word, and that came in handy sometimes—as was still true all these years later. I paid him well, but he lived in a simple home and dressed plainly. He wasn't married and seemed to have no interests other than serving as my steward and doing whatever I asked of him. Today, that meant visiting Joseph's workshop, an hour and a half's walk to the south, to see if he had hired anyone or was still working by himself.

When James returned that afternoon, he said Joseph was alone, except for his son.

"Was the boy doing anything?" I asked. "Or just watching?"

James checked his writing tablet before answering. He took notes on everything. "He hammered some nails, but that was all."

In hindsight, I should have put Joseph out of business then and there. It would have saved me a lot of trouble later. But I let it go. I was expanding into Cana at the time, so I was often on the road. And Martha was with child—John, my firstborn son—and I was building a new home (the one before where we now live). I had bigger things to think about than a few stools.

Years passed, and my business continued to flourish. The Romans hired me to build a stable in Capernaum, and that opened up a multitude of new opportunities for me—everything from crosses to courthouses. My laborers grumbled about working for Romans, but I had no interest in politics. Silver was silver.

Life was just as good at home. Martha gave birth to our daughter, Elizabeth, and my second son, Luke. I bought land on the highest hill in Sepphoris and built a mansion almost worthy of Solomon, with eight rooms, mosaic floors, and indoor baths. As James said, the greatest builder in Galilee should have the finest house. Same for the garden. I filled it with lilies and roses and all manner of fruits: figs, dates, pomegranates, apples. And olives, of course. I hired a servant to care for it full-time. Maybe my father used to tend a garden like mine. I would have enjoyed ordering him around.

So I had little reason to think about Joseph. I bumped into him occasionally if he had a job here in town, but we rarely spoke. Then James told me one morning that Joseph had died. He'd been sick for a long time—some sort of palsy.

I stopped listening. Construction on a wall I was building in Magdala was running behind schedule, and I couldn't afford any more delays.

"His son is taking over his shop," James said.

This made me pause. He was just one carpenter in a lowly village, but you could never be too careful. "Keep an eye on him," I said.

* * *

Then it came to pass that James said he needed to show me something at the synagogue. I hadn't stepped foot inside it in months and didn't plan on returning until the next high holiday. I'd suffered through enough services as a boy, thanks to my father. He earned practically nothing as a gardener, but every week he'd tithe a fifth of his wages—double what the scriptures required. Every night when we weren't at the synagogue, he'd read aloud from the Torah to my brothers and me while my mother mended holes in our threadbare tunics. So I'd had my fill of religion and the poverty that came with it. If my competitors wanted to waste their time at services, good for them. They'd be working for me soon anyway.

The synagogue was badly in need of repair; no doubt the priests were pocketing the tithes for themselves. The roof leaked, the benches wobbled, and the holy ark—a cabinet built into a recess in the wall that held the Torah scrolls—was on the verge of falling apart. Even a nonbeliever like myself found it embarrassing. If it had been up to me, I'd have torn the whole structure down and rebuilt it. But as soon as James brought me inside, I knew what he wanted me to see. The ark had been replaced, and the new one was astonishing.

It had two doors that opened from the center, like the old one, and was the same size as the original. But the craftsmanship was flawless. I reached out to touch it, then drew short. There was something strange about it—almost as if it had been there forever, and the synagogue constructed around it.

"Joseph's son," James said. "He donated it."

So that was my second sign. I knew then that I'd been right about Philip's stools: Joseph hadn't built them after all. But I never guessed it was his boy. Where'd he been hiding all these years? Waiting for Joseph to die? It didn't make sense. But whatever his reason for lying low in the past, he must have cast it aside. If you were an up-and-coming carpenter and wanted to show off your talent, the synagogue was the place to do it. I had to admit, it was a cunning move. I should have thought of it myself.

If I didn't act quickly, this boy could be a thorn in my side for many years to come.

* * *

With his short legs, James took three steps for every two of mine. "This way," he said, pointing left as we entered the village.

I'd been to Nazareth many times, most recently for a cousin's wedding. I could see why Joseph liked it here: nothing but average people, living unexceptional lives. Salt of the earth, the rabbis called them. The sooner I could leave, the better.

I smelled bread baking in an oven as we passed a communal kitchen. All these little villages had them; each one served several families. Near the entrance, an old blind man sat with his back to the trunk of an olive tree. When he heard us approaching, he started banging his cup with a stick, begging for money. We ignored him, and James turned right, proceeded about fifty cubits, then stopped in front of a modest workshop. Tools were arranged neatly on a bench. A table displayed a few items for sale: a small wooden box, a carved horse, some household utensils.

Joseph's son was unloading a cypress bough from a wagon when we arrived, so he didn't notice us at first. He was no more than thirty, medium build, and unremarkable in every way. Not ugly, but not handsome, either. His commonness disappointed me. This was the master carpenter? I wondered if James had directed me to the wrong man until, lo, he swung his axe into the limb and cleaved it in half. And I mean exactly in half. He laid the two pieces side by side; neither was a hair longer than the other.

"You have great talent," I said.

He looked up, and I had the feeling he already knew me. But then, most laborers in Galilee would have recognized Timothy the builder. He struck twice again with his axe, and now there were four pieces, all the same length. "My father taught me well," he said.

"No offense to Joseph. He was a diligent worker and a righteous man. But you're twice the carpenter that he ever was."

He set one of the four pieces on a table and, selecting an adze from his collection of tools, began stripping away the bark. He worked deliberately, but no motion was wasted.

"A man with your skill could do very well for himself if the right opportunity came along," I said. Again, no answer. My heart began to harden. If he truly recognized me, then he knew I deserved respect.

My thoughts were interrupted by two young men passing by. One grabbed his companion by the arm, and they stopped to talk. The first man said he'd been a good son. He worked hard and looked after his father—not like his older brother, who'd demanded his inheritance, squandered all his money on wine and whores, then came crawling back, begging for mercy.

Joseph's son paused to listen as the young man raised his voice. His father gave his brother a feast! He served him a fatted calf! Why should he have to settle for scraps while his good-for-nothing brother stuffed his belly?

The men moved on, and Joseph's son returned to his adze, but the story gave me an idea.

"Your father blessed you with something much greater

than a calf," I said. "He taught you a trade. And now he'd want you to use that trade to care for your mother."

His pace slowed, just for an instant, then resumed. I had found his weakness. "Come work for me," I said. "You'll oversee all my laborers, in every village. You'll never have to lift an adze again, and your mother will have whatever she needs until the end of her days."

He was tempted, I could tell. But then he stood, stiff-necked, to face me. "I must carry on my father's business," he said.

James, behind me, drew in his breath sharply. Anger filled my heart. I had come to this young carpenter in a spirit of kindness, with an offer most men would die for, and this was how he repaid me? I was accustomed to such arrogance from physicians and lawyers, but I'd be damned if I took it from a common grain of salt.

I smiled at him coldly. "Then I wish you success."

As I turned to leave, I noticed the little box among his wares and picked it up. Oak and square, it was the length of my hand and half as deep. And light as a dove but so sturdy that I could have used it as a hammer. The lid slid along grooves—a simple design, but I'd never seen it wrought so skillfully in a box this small. If I could produce it in bulk, I'd make a tenfold profit off each one, and he'd never sell another again. "I've taken much of your time," I said. "Let me buy this as a token of my thanks."

"If you like it, please take it." He spoke to me as if I were a child.

I opened my bag of silver and removed two coins. "Trust

me, I can afford to pay."

"Thank you, but I have no need of your money."

I dropped the entire bag on the table. "Everyone needs money." The bag contained more silver than he could earn in a year, but he refused even to glance at it.

"I know this manner of man," I told James on our way back to Sepphoris. "He's already in his house, where no one else can see, counting the coins one by one."

And he'd know: That money came from me.

* * *

When I returned home, Martha was sitting on a bench in the garden with a tunic in her lap, watching over the children. John dozed under a fig tree. Elizabeth marched a doll through an imaginary scene while Luke tossed pebbles in the air and counted how many he could catch. It was too peaceful to last. Sure enough, tiring of his game, Luke threw a pebble at the doll and knocked it over. Elizabeth punched him in the shoulder, and he whimpered.

If only Elizabeth were a boy. I couldn't imagine either son ever running my business.

Martha made room for me on the bench, and I sat next to her. She asked about my day, but before I could answer, Luke spotted the box in my hands and hurried over to inspect it. He had already forgotten about his shoulder.

"What do you think of it?" I asked.

He opened the lid, dropped his pebbles inside, and closed it up. The pebbles made a joyful noise when he shook the box, and he laughed. "Like a timbrel," he said. "Can I have it?"

Elizabeth grabbed the box out of his hands and dumped out the pebbles. Her doll fit inside it snugly. "This could be her bed!" she exclaimed. Even John roused himself and demanded to hold it.

Their reactions provoked me. I had built them this mansion with this beautiful garden, and the only thing that impressed them was a wooden box.

"It's lovely," Martha said. She, too, had fallen under its spell. "Did one of your workers make it?" She removed the doll and replaced it with a spool of thread that I hadn't noticed before. So that's why the tunic was on her lap; she'd been repairing it. I employed four maidservants, yet Martha did their work for them, as if she were married to a gardener.

I grabbed the spool from the box and held it in the air between us. "Don't we have servants?" I asked.

"I enjoy it. And what else would I do all day while you're traveling across Galilee?"

"I travel across Galilee so no one in my family will ever have to sew."

She made a sound between a laugh and a groan. "Right. I keep forgetting."

I was too vexed to argue with her. I took the box and went inside to a private room where I could be alone. Where had this carpenter gained such skill? Not from Joseph, verily. I slid the top of the box open and closed and open again, searching for its secret. I hadn't built anything with my own hands in many years. But even at my best, could I have matched it?

I pushed the question aside. I had chosen my path long ago, and I had no regrets. Anyone could be a carpenter, but I employed dozens of them. Tomorrow I would speak to James.

* * *

Three weeks went by. While I waited, I bought a vineyard near Tiberias. James found it for me. I was running out of ways to expand my construction business, and I already supplied other vineyards with barrels and presses. So it was a shrewd decision financially—not to mention something that no carpenter from Nazareth would ever accomplish.

Then it came to pass one morning that James placed four boxes on a table in the garden: the one from Joseph's son and, lined up in a row, three others of the same size. I put a few pebbles in the first one and shook it; the rattle was dull and somber, so I set it aside. The second box was too heavy; I didn't even open it.

The last was the most beautiful of the three. My hopes rose; this would be the one. But when I placed Elizabeth's doll inside, the box wouldn't close.

"These three were the best of them?" I asked.

"Yes," James said quietly.

All over Galilee, my carpenters were beginning their labors. They went wherever I commanded them to go and built whatever I commanded them to build. But not him. I felt like a shepherd with a hundred sheep until one wandered away. No matter where I searched or how loudly I called, it refused to come. The other ninety-nine meant nothing to me; all I wanted was the one I couldn't have.

Someone needed to suffer for this. If not Joseph's son, someone else. I swept the three boxes off the table.

James looked at me, his dark eyes full of sorrow. He

leaned over to pick up the box closest to him, pinning it between his left arm and torso. When he tucked the second box next to it, both slipped through his grasp and dropped to the ground. Sighing, he gathered them and set them on the table. Then he retrieved the third one, returned it to the table, and stacked all three, topping them with his tablet. Lifting the stack from the bottom, he leaned it against his chest and secured it with his chin. His sandals scraped the ground as he slowly left my sight, afraid to lift his feet for fear of dropping the boxes all over again.

Alone now, I walked to the southern edge of the garden. Sepphoris lay below me. Wherever I looked, I saw my handiwork: houses, walls, gates, towers. I had built them to last for generations. And in the distance, beyond my vision, was Nazareth.

Everyone had a price. He was no different than anyone else.

* * *

This time, I traveled without James. I wanted to have this conversation alone.

The old blind man was under the same tree, still banging his cup. His sandals seemed new, but perhaps I had overlooked them on my earlier visit. Either way, he didn't need my charity.

When I arrived at the shop, the carpenter was speaking to a small group of men gathered in a half circle around him. I stood a few cubits apart, close enough to listen.

"There was a certain man who owned a vineyard," he said.

I gasped. Was he speaking about me? How did he know

I'd bought one? But he continued his story; he meant someone else, of course. This man, he said, hired some workers early in the morning and offered to pay each one a denarius. Later, he hired more workers, and in the afternoon, still more. When the sun set, all received the same wage: a denarius.

The man nearest me interrupted. He had broad shoulders with a sunburned neck and looked as if he'd labored in his share of vineyards. "That's not fair," he said. "Those who worked longer should get more pay."

"Let's ask our visitor," the carpenter said. "What do you think, Timothy?"

The others turned toward me, and I felt the weight of their stares. Suddenly I was back in Torah school, a young boy again, struggling to name the twelve tribes of Israel while my classmates laughed at me behind their hands. I shook off the memory and spoke with a confidence I didn't feel.

"Did the owner pay each man the amount he agreed to work for?"

"He did."

"Then the workers have no cause to complain."

He nodded at me and smiled. "Timothy is right," he said. "It's the owner's money. He can do with it what he will."

I felt a gladness in my heart that confounded me, and I chastised myself. Of course I had answered correctly. I didn't need this young carpenter's approval. When had he ever hired any workers? I was the only master here.

The others soon departed, leaving the two of us. Joseph's son turned his attention to a piece of limestone and prepared to cut it. I didn't know why he bothered; nothing would come of such a worthless stone.

"Have you reconsidered my offer?" I asked. He picked up a chisel but didn't answer. With no more customers around, his arrogance had returned. "You know I'm a wealthy man."

He smote the stone, and a piece fell to the ground. "Indeed," he said at last. "And my neighbors are grateful. Thanks to your silver, the hungry were fed, the homeless have shelter, the poor have new clothes."

A moment passed before I realized what he meant. "That money was for you," I said.

"Yes, but the owner can do whatever he wants with it, don't you agree?" He smiled as if pleased with himself. "You think I took the credit for helping those people? And then when they need a craftsman, they'll hire me instead of one of your workers?"

I wanted to deny it but could not. He chiseled off another piece of stone.

"I told them the money came from Timothy of Sepphoris, the builder."

Was he possessed by devils? What would it gain him to praise a rival? Then, in an instant, I understood. He knew he could never equal what I had achieved. As hard as he labored, and even with his great skill, he would never be more than a common carpenter. So he pretended that he had no need of worldly possessions, that he was happier poor and unknown than I would ever be with my wealth and fame. That's why he rejected my offer to provide for his mother. That's why he gave away my silver. He was trying to turn the tables on me. To make me covet his way of life. But I was on to him now.

* * *

The next morning, I explained my plan to James. I would send my two best laborers to Nazareth. If Joseph's son charged six denarii to build a wall, they should charge three. They could even work for free. I'd make up the difference in their wages. Whatever it took to drive him out of business and out of my life. James wrote down my instructions in silence. If he disagreed with me, he knew better than to say so. Not after failing me with the boxes.

My laborers were soon busy in Nazareth while Joseph's son worked less and less. Within a week, James reported, no one was hiring him at all.

"What does he do all day while my workers are taking his wages?" I pointed to James's tablet. "Read it to me."

"He tells stories," James said. "People gather at his shop to listen." He read from his notes. "One was about a buried treasure. A certain man found it in a field, but he didn't want anyone to know about it. So he saved up all his money and—"

I cut him off. First vineyards, now buried treasures. I had no patience for stories. "Does he try to sell them anything? Has he made any more boxes?"

"No," James said, "the people just asked him questions and he answered them. Or sometimes he asked them questions."

"He's up to something," I said. "Find out what it is."

The next morning, James reported that the crowd had grown. Entire families attended, even little children. "He stood on a table so everyone could hear him. He talked about a king who held a wedding banquet for his son and invited—"

I held up my hand. "Again, he did no work?"

"None."

"Does he ask anyone for money? Or food?"

James shook his head.

It made no sense. How long could he last without wages? Telling stories wouldn't feed his mother.

"If you wish," James said, "I could return to his workshop today and see."

He was facing the sun, so his eyes were narrowed and wrinkled at the corners. His tightly curled hair had turned gray, but he was still James the Lesser, still my faithful disciple. I wondered how long he would have waited until I answered. An hour? All morning? My heart was moved; I shouldn't have made him pick up those boxes.

"Yes," I said. "Go."

* * *

But, lo, James didn't return the next morning. This had never happened before. He was in good health and knew I was expecting a report. Was his head so filled with buried treasures and wedding banquets that he'd forgotten who he worked for?

Hours passed. I tried to occupy myself with other matters. My vineyard was producing only half the yield that I'd been promised, and I should have summoned the steward to provide an account. But I couldn't stop thinking about Joseph's son. Why was he gathering customers to his shop if not to sell them goods? Did he have some other source of income? Then I remembered my bag of silver, and suddenly I understood. He hadn't given it all away—he'd only pretended to do so while hoarding the largest portion for himself. He was a hypocrite, no better than the priests at the synagogue! And oh, how he must be laughing at me, living like a king with my money.

I put on my cloak and set out to confront him face-to-face. I walked quickly, my anger burning hotter with each step. I would hear no more of his stories, no more clever words that troubled my heart. He would return my silver and depart from Galilee at once, or I would beat him until his dying breath.

But when I arrived at his shop, no one was there. The table was empty, and the tools had vanished.

An elderly man walked by, muttering to himself as if possessed. I called to him. "The carpenter—have you seen him?"

The man began laughing for no reason and pointing here and there. "I see the house, I see the tree, I see the sky, I see—"

I grabbed him roughly by the shoulders. "Joseph's son. Where is he?"

"I don't know." He was still laughing. "I saw him yesterday, but I don't see him today."

I shoved him aside, and the old man staggered away. Had I won? I wanted the carpenter of Nazareth to leave, and, lo, he had departed. But where was he now? Perhaps he had moved to another village to open a new shop. Yes, that must be it. He said he wanted to continue his father's business—he must have fled somewhere he thought he could escape me. If so, he was mistaken. Did he not know how far my reach extended? All my workers, in every village, would watch for him. Wherever the sheep wandered, I would track him down.

And if he continued to defy me? What would I do then? My thoughts turned violent as I pondered the price he would pay.

I wished then that I could speak with James. He had observed the carpenter many times; perhaps he could discern where he was hiding. Again, I wondered why he didn't come to my garden this morning. Could he have already begun the hunt? Of course! That was the only possible explanation. As soon as he'd discovered the carpenter was missing, he must have set out to look for him. He might be with him at this very moment.

Good man, James. No one was more loyal. A friend, even. I would discuss the matter with him tomorrow. He would surely return tomorrow.

* * *

Discussion Questions

1. Timothy the builder has a specific perspective and life focus. How would you describe it? Is he unique or wrong to have that perspective and life focus? What are the benefits and detriments of his life focus?
2. On several occasions, Timothy the builder incorrectly interprets the motivations of Joseph's son. Why is Timothy unable to understand the young carpenter's motivations?
3. What characteristic allows certain individuals to be better (*or worse*) at perspective shifting?
4. What could Timothy the builder have done to better understand and believe the motivations of Joseph's son rather than continuing to see them through his own perspective?
5. Is it wrong to simply want to work, become successful, and take care of your family as Timothy has done? Why is Timothy an unsympathetic character in this story?

* * *

What We Talk About When We Talk About Reincarnation

Edward Daschle

* * *

My boyfriend, Mike, was talking, just really going on like he was delivering a lecture in one of his economics classes. He's twice my age, so he thinks that gives him the right.

Our friends call us Michael squared when they think they're being cute, but we're safe around Jaime and Amy since their names rhyme. Amy was my friend, and Jaime was Mike's, and it was the two of them who'd introduced the two of us, though not with any intention that we'd begin dating. We were just two guests at the same party they'd been hosting. Sometimes I felt this, more than anything else, was what kept us all as a set. There was little else we really had in common. Mike and I only drink wine, but since Jaime and Amy brought the drinks, what we had was beer. The bottles we'd already emptied crowded the table under the light, and I was trying to decide if they were amber or just brown while Mike got himself worked up over the history of reincarnation. He'd made his way through literature and metaphysics and ended up in a cul-de-sac of science fiction. He doesn't believe in anything he calls woo-woo or what anyone else would call spiritual, though there is a little Buddha nestled between a few books in the living room.

The apartment is Mike's, and his furnishings are to die for. I don't remember what we ate or drank the first time he invited me over, but I do remember the mid-century modern Danish chairs, futon, and cabinet, the tastefully minimalist, queer paintings, and the small statement sculptures on his shelves and the coffee table. His, I recognized in this first glimpse, was a life well-organized and not one spent on anyone else. He had constructed himself, too, in a way, through daily workouts and tight shirts, a neatly trimmed beard to deemphasize his age, and the gold-rimmed glasses he preferred over contacts. When we officialized our relationship by telling our friends and touching each other delicately in public the way couples do, he became my safety net, a personification of the concept of security. Already, I'd been thinking of him as something of a template for who I'd like to become. I'd decided, not so explicitly at first, though certainly it was a decision, once I reach his age, once he's passed and I have my own apartment overlooking the water and a boyfriend half my age, I will shorten my name to Mike and carry on his legacy of good taste.

"Hey, who do you think you were in a past life?" Jaime asked.

It took all of Jaime's burly force to interrupt Mike. Jaime was built like a Tolkienesque dwarf, looking as though nobody would ever be able to push him over. He'd transitioned only recently. Sometimes I guiltily felt that talking to him was a pronoun minefield, though on the couple occasions I slipped up, he said nothing. For a brief period when I was younger, I thought I might like to be a girl. I'd never told anyone this, and it didn't matter, because I did not feel that I was trans or at least not that I could live as a trans woman. It was just an idle thought, and I figured if there were an afterlife where I could choose how I would turn out in my next life, I would probably not choose to be a boy again. Biologically anyways. I wondered if it was fucked up to think along these lines, if this reinforced the notion of who was a real woman and who wasn't, but I wasn't about to have that conversation here, not now. It wasn't a beer conversation, something so delicate. Maybe it was a conversation I could only have with a therapist since Mike would condescend, not cruelly, but only out of years of experience in entertaining fruitless hypotheticals and out of his own misgivings over the complexities of gender identity.

Jaime said that in a past life, he figured he was nobody special. He'd never won any awards growing up—the only statistically unusual thing about him being the fact that he was a trans man. He'd probably worked, ate, shit, and then died of something stupid like a toothache.

"Though considering I have you now, I must've done something right in my last life," Jaime said to Amy in a voice that sounded like he was talking to a dog. Though I hadn't yet said it aloud, I did love Mike, but I would hate to hear my own voice dribble so mushily from my mouth.

"I think in a past life, I was Galileo," Amy said.

"Galileo?" Jaime asked.

"I just think I have a connection to him; I did a report on him in first grade."

"What?"

"On Galileo, Michael, you remember, right? We had to choose a scientist, and then our teacher was fired for spreading secular beliefs."

I laughed.

"No, I don't remember any of that," I said, "but that's kind of hilarious. I can't believe they fired, what was her name—Ms. Miller, right?—over something like that."

"You can't?" Mike asked. "I can believe it completely."

"You know what I mean. Sure, it was a Catholic school, but seriously, besides the uniform, it was more or less normal, I think," I said. "And I don't know, things like that... they just always seem to happen somewhere else."

I looked around at the others. Amy shrugged.

"But why Galileo?" Jaime asked. "I mean there's more to it than a report, isn't there?"

"It's stupid, but I guess he just always sort of stuck with me. He's like my own personal inspirational quote. Like 'hang in there, Amy, at least you aren't imprisoned,'" she said.

I laughed again, but Jaime, I could see, looked thoughtful.

"But you were imprisoned in a way," Jaime said. "You had to hide yourself. I basically had to break down that closet door with an axe."

"And I'm glad you did," Amy said, tilting her head gently

so that it touched Jaime's. "But I don't want to blame my parents for that. I mean, they gave me everything and they loved me, even if I couldn't always, you know, say everything to them."

Jaime wrapped an arm tightly around Amy's shoulders, pulling her into his side.

Amy's parents adopted her when she was old enough to be grateful but young enough not to be bitter about the whole system. We've had conversations about what that means to her. Once, she told me how she had this feeling that if she wasn't perfect, they'd get buyer's remorse and question her adoptee warranty. It was why she'd taken longer than I had to renounce the faith in which we'd both been raised. She still considered herself to be a spiritual person, and sometimes her social media posts made me wonder if she didn't need something to fill the space the church had left behind.

"You are perfect. Anyone who could reject you just doesn't know you," Jaime said.

Mike, I could tell, wanted to say something. Maybe how that wasn't true. How there were plenty of people who would reject you because they knew you, but I reached across and squeezed his thigh gently to shut him up. He set his warm hand on mine.

"All right, Mike, let's hear it," Jaime said smugly and resignedly, ready it seemed for something longwinded. He was leaning back again, the thin-armed chair looking entirely too delicate to contain his swagger, the empty beer bottles before him forming a crenulated parapet. "And I don't want to hear any sort of theory or anything like that. Just pretend, for a moment, that reincarnation exists in the way most people understand that it does."

"Fine, fine," Mike said, in that fake exhausted voice he sometimes uses, the voice I hate because it reminds me how much older he is, how in the wrong light he looks like my dad. "Actually, my first boyfriend totally bought into all that spiritual bullshit. This was back in the early '80s when things like psychics were on their way out, barely holding onto the market share they'd scratched out for themselves in the '60s and '70s. I was a skeptic, but I was also smitten, just over the moon for him. He was so brave and out there and sexy too. I'm not ashamed to say he was my first love, and first love really makes you do crazy things. I was practically a different person from the bitter old faggot you see before you now. What I mean is, I was willing to believe anything he believed in, no matter how crazy I really thought it was.

"So he had this psychic he went to, and one time he took me to see her. She had on all this eye makeup and loads of shawls and things. At the time, I thought she was really old, though now I think that was just the effect she was going for—you know, to make herself seem wiser and more mysterious—she probably wasn't much over forty at the time." Mike lifted his beer to his lips, but didn't take a drink, just held it there before his face almost as though he'd been petrified, the Medusa gaze of memory holding him fast. I held my own second beer, though I'd already decided I wouldn't finish it, not with all those empty calories. I couldn't afford them, not if Mike was going to think about an old boyfriend. I didn't like the look he had in his eyes. Or maybe I was just jealous he wasn't looking that way at me.

He blinked, took a drink, and then set the beer back on the table.

"He asked her to tell us about our past lives, if we'd been lovers then like we were at the time. Apparently, this was the main service she provided. Anyway, she told us that she saw something—she put on this misty voice—and for his sake, I really tried to let myself buy into it. Later though, after the first time we broke up, I promised I'd never pretend to believe in bullshit for a guy again, no matter how hot he was. I did, I believed in a lot of bullshit, but I got more suspicious each time. She said why yes, the two of us were, but things ended tragically.

Maybe she knew fags loved melodrama, or maybe she was picking up on something else, but that really got him, and me too by proxy. She said we'd been in boarding school together in the 1910s. We had a clandestine relationship. He'd had to put off the girls his parents tried to set him up with, and I was always finding new ways to sneak into his room when his roommate was out. Very *Maurice* and *A Separate Peace*. But then the war started, and there we were, me English and him German—it could've been the other way around, but I guess she noticed a sort of Teutonic intensity in him, which is probably why she was in the business she was in, the way she picked up on things like that. We fought on opposite sides of the war, memories of each other were all that kept us alive in the trenches. But then, when in the heat of battle, we didn't recognize each other, all covered in trench mud and wearing our uniforms, we fought, and I killed him. Only as he lay dying in my arms did I realize who he was. I died not long after from sepsis or something else ugly and painful.

"That's what she told us, anyway."

"I'm going to have to talk to that psychic," Jaime said. "Do you think she's still alive?"

"I don't know," Mike said. "But Harvey died seven years after that."

We could hear the rush hour traffic on the street far below, but that was all we could hear. I kept expecting someone to break the silence before realizing it had to be me. "How did he die? You've never talked about him before."

I felt so impotent. I was always thinking about how even if our relationship ended with Mike's death of old age, barring unreasonable longevity, we would be together for less than half his life. It's disconcerting, sometimes, to think how long I'll be left alone.

"How do you think?" Mike asked, but the gruffness was only playacting. It was a bad actor's attempt at putting on the anger the script asked for. It was well-worn and cliché.

"So, it was AIDS," Jaime said, and I could see Amy tense up beside him. "That fucking sucks. It's always fucking AIDS. You know, my uncle died of AIDS. I was young when he passed; this was in the early '90s. I just remember him being all thin, pale, and wrung-out looking. His lips were dry and looked like the Salt Flats in Utah near where my grandparents lived. I was certain he'd been cursed since I was really into mummies at the time."

"It's always fucking AIDS," Mike agreed. "He died in '89. I don't really want to get into everything, but it was just as terrible as you're imagining. I wasn't there as much as I know I should've been, but I was young, and all he was doing was dying. He didn't have any family with him either; they'd decided to forget him before we even met. When I did visit, he just kept repeating that bullshit story the psychic told us. I think that's why I still remember it. There were times when I was certain he couldn't tell the difference between what was real and what was the story. He didn't just believe that he'd lived that past life; he believed he was living it out in that hospital. He even tried to speak German a few times. But he didn't know German, so he just muttered a few made-up phrases in the worst fake accent I've ever heard. I had to work so hard not to laugh, even with all those men dying around him."

The sky began to orange and then purple, blooming like a flower or like a bruise, considering the topic of the conversation. Mike's furniture cast spidery shadows across the floor, and just for a moment, before Jaime shifted, the light caught in the empty bottles on the table, refilling them.

"What month did he die?" I asked.

"What month...?" Mike asked, still smiling off the end of his sad laughter. "It would've been... August? Yeah, fucking terrible month. He thought he was freezing to death, but I was boiling in that shitty apartment we used to share."

"I was born in September that year," I said. I was speaking quietly because even as I spoke, I knew I probably shouldn't be saying what I was saying. But I couldn't help it; the topic of the evening had caught hold of me. "You know how that psychic was talking about lovers in past lives? Maybe he was my past life, and that's why we're..."

Mike stared at me, eyes seeming to reach right to the

edges of his gold-rimmed glasses.

"You know, I just thought there would be something magical about that, and considering the coincidence," I said, "of when he died and I was born... it just fits, I guess."

We stopped breathing, all of us. Amy and Jaime were still; Mike stony beside me.

"It's all bullshit," Mike said finally without force. "The psychic, reincarnation, all of it. And I hate the idea of soulmates. The world's too big for soulmates and any of that bullshit. You shouldn't need to believe someone is your only choice to fall in love with them. You should just be able to love or lust or whatever else. I mean, Jesus Christ, none of that is necessary. It's just about compatibility and making it work. Fighting to make it work if you have to."

I set my hand back on Mike's knee, and though his body was warm, all I felt was coldness when he didn't set his hand on mine.

"Soulmates scare me," Amy said.

"How do you mean?" Jaime asked.

"It just seems so easy for two people to never meet and then your souls would never be fulfilled. I mean, sorry Michael, but Mike is twice your age. I don't think you ever expected to end up with him. And what if there are rules to soulmates we don't know?"

"Jesus," Mike muttered. He was done with the conversation.

"But maybe that's what reincarnation is all about," Jaime said. "Correcting mistakes made by another you in another life. Maybe we just keep coming back until we find our soulmates."

"Or maybe it doesn't mean anything at all, and it's just something our ancestors made up because their lives were shit, their world was shit, and every day they were starving and depressed," Mike said.

The cats screamed just then from the bedroom.

"Oh, shit, forgot to feed the bastards," Mike said and went to let them out. We always keep them in the bedroom whenever we have guests over, even, or maybe especially, guests who like cats. It's not that we're concerned about the cats being a nuisance, they are nice enough as far as cats go, but guests are always making a nuisance out of themselves around cats. Some people are allergic to cats, but the real issue is how the cats derail conversations. They come into the room, and there we go spending an evening talking about cats instead of whatever it was we were talking about before the cats entered the picture.

And in they came, mewing up at each of us. Jaime nabbed the orange one we called Marmalade when we weren't calling him Stinker, and though Amy wiggled her fingers at Alfredo, he sauntered off into the kitchen after Mike, more interested in food than attention for the time being.

"You know, cats have nine lives," I said.

"So they say," Jaime said while he scratched behind Marmalade's ears. "Hey, can we get...?"

"Hey, Mike? Can you grab a few more beers? So, is it reincarnation," I asked, "when a cat dies, and they use another life? Or is it more like Mario, and they just get to try again?"

"I hadn't really thought of it that way, but now that you mention it, I guess I would probably say it's more like Mario,"

Amy said.

"But what if it were reincarnation?" I asked. "How many cats are actually running about in the world? I mean, how many have there ever been?"

"Nine times fewer than we think, I guess," Jaime said.

"No, but seriously," I said, "what if reincarnation doesn't obey the laws of space and time, you know? I mean if we're going spiritual anyways, there's no reason to believe that a cat with nine lives has to live those lives back-to-back like dominoes. Oops, got ran over, there's one down. Oops, got eaten by a coyote, there's another—"

"Michael," Mike warned as he returned to us with what would turn out to be the last round of beers. He's sensitive to talk about the cats dying. He grew up in California, where his family had practically been feeding the coyotes with the cats they brought home from the shelter.

"So, Mike's—our—two cats might actually be the same cat reincarnated into the same place and time in two different bodies," I continued. "In a few years, when one... passes... it will go on to the great kitty beyond and then get its next life and reincarnate a few years before now as the second cat. Just like that. Or maybe one cat is the first life, and the other is the seventh or something. So maybe the sixth life experienced the end of the world or was a sabretooth tiger."

Marmalade leapt from Jaime's lap to join his brother in the kitchen.

"You know, I kind of lied earlier." Amy admitted.

"What about?"

"About who I thought I was in a past life. I mean, about

why I thought I was who I was," she said. "I did do a report on Galileo and all, but actually it has more to do with that Indigo Girls song. I went to one of their concerts with an ex—sorry honey—and I felt like I was experiencing destiny. Like I did a report on Galileo, and there they were singing about him."

"Oh fuck, major lesbian credentials alert!" Jaime said, jabbing the air repeatedly with his index fingers like an insistent sign pointing Amy out.

"Destiny and reincarnation? I feel like there's something there," I said.

"Actually, hey, I have a theory. My theory is that having a child is the closest thing we have to reincarnation," Jaime said. I noticed he and Amy exchanged a meaningful look.

"Really? Come on," Mike said. "That's so hetero. It's such a straight belief to think that having children is anything like reincarnation. It's completely toxic. My parents had that sort of feeling about me and then hated when I didn't turn out just like them."

"You know I actually don't disagree with you there?" Jaime said, and Amy nodded. "Like it's fucked, yeah, but I was thinking more biologically speaking. There's genetic memory and all that shit. I read something about how stress can be passed down through generations."

"Plus, you're talking about expectations, right? Not really reincarnation," Amy said. "My parents aren't my biological parents, but they had expectations."

"Sure, fine," Mike said. "But it's still fucking hetero to think of your child as any sort of extension of you. They aren't beholden to you. Like do you think you owe your past lives anything? I mean, obviously not because reincarnation isn't real, but it's the same with children. Just let them be their own person. Maybe we should just stop having kids for a bit, like as a society, until we get our messed-up shit sorted out."

"You're going to hate this then, but Amy and I have something kind of big to tell you."

Jaime loves saying he has something big to tell you. Those were the same words he used to come out as trans, and likely how he'd announced he was a lesbian in a previous life, years before he and Amy started dating. But, though occasionally he chases this phrase with truly momentous news, mostly it's exaggeration, and we all get to roll our eyes at his idea of scope.

"We're planning to get pregnant," he said.

Mike and I didn't have to exchange looks, though in a sitcom, we would have, very urgently and dramatically. We'd both been blindsided, and neither one of us knew quite what to say about this.

"Congratulations!" I said.

"Living that hetero fantasy!" Mike said. "Fantastic!"

"That's not—" Amy said.

"As a queer couple, anything we decide to do is inherently queer," Jaime said. "Anyways, I'm the one getting pregnant."

"Yeah, okay, okay," Mike said. "Oh, wait, hold on, back it up. How's that?"

"I've always wanted to be a mom," Amy said, tone halfway between apologetic and staunch, "but getting pregnant, going through all that, and then the time I'd have to take off from work... it just doesn't appeal to me. But you know, before Jaime came out, we weren't considering having a kid at all. It wasn't even on our radar."

"It's because I wasn't being who I am yet, if that's not chronologically confusing," Jaime said. "I had to kill whoever that bitch was—"

"Honey," Amy said lightly. She'd fallen for that bitch after all.

"Sorry, but I mean, going back to reincarnation again," Jaime said, picking up his empty bottle, not remembering he'd already emptied it. "I couldn't even conceive of being a parent in that past life because being a parent meant being a mother. But now, my soul and mind are aligned, and I can be the father I was always meant to be."

"Soul and mind," Mike repeated with a hint of derision, whether over the spirituality of the sentiment or over the absence of "body" in the equation. "But you're a man now, right?"

"I've always been a man," Jaime said. "It just took me some time to figure myself out."

"Hmmm," Mike said and finished off his third beer.

"What?" Jaime asked.

"It's just you were a lesbian, and now you're planning to have a kid, so was it really always?" Mike asked. They'd had this sort of discussion before to varying degrees. When Jaime came out as trans, Mike had had any number of questions, only a few of which he'd asked Jaime and a few more he'd ranted about to me later. He was from a different generation, I'd explained to Amy, the two of us acting as wartime negotiators when our partners argued over identity.

"Don't give me that bullshit," Jaime said. Amy's fingers jolted in a warning caress across Jaime's shoulders. "Look, identity's fluid, and we're all always just trying to figure ourselves out. I mean, come on, dude, no need to be transphobic."

"Transphobic? What the hell," Mike said. He never raises his voice just increases the pressure. "I'm the fag who lived through the AIDS epidemic here. Look, I'm just saying you can't have it both ways. You can't expect people to think of you as a man if you plan to get pregnant. And hey, this isn't really about you. I'm just tired of people making up new identities now because they want to be special. We didn't live through all that bullshit so that the next generation of dykes and fags could find new ways to be discriminated against. Jesus Christ. You can be a masculine lesbian without being trans. Identity doesn't have to be so binary as—"

"Fucking binary? I'm a man, and I'm having a baby! Fuck!" Jaime shouted, though he was still leaning back in his chair.

"How would you define a man then?" Mike asked. "Can you even define a woman anymore?"

"If I started to define *woman*, you'd just pull out a plucked chicken and say 'behold, a woman!'"

I laughed. Somehow, I was laughing. As much as I didn't want to push on Mike's ego or test the already strained flex of the evening, I was laughing, imagining a woman-sized plucked chicken, taking calls in an office, walking about in heels, wearing lipstick. As though heels and lipstick were what anyone might use to define a woman.

"Sorry," I said. "I was just imagining..."

They were all looking at me, and for a moment, I wondered if this would be enough. Mike always apologized in the end when he went too far—he was always taking things as far as he could. But even so, I wondered when the end would be too late, when Jaime or Amy would decide to put the story down before they got there, and if too late might've just passed us by.

"Jesus," Mike whispered. And then looked back up at Jaime, earnestness in his eyes. "Hey, congratulations on the whole baby thing. Forget I said anything. So how are you doing it? Are you going to bust out the old turkey baster?"

He'd toted out that old gag, the clumsiness itself an attempt at an apology.

"You know, it's getting late," Jaime said. "We should get out of here."

"Oh, come on," Mike said. "It's still rush hour. Stay a bit."

"I have this great aged cheese I found at the market. We could have some of that while we wait for traffic to calm down," I said.

Maybe if I were worried about karma, I'd have tried harder to mend the rupture before our guests left respectively angry and disappointed. But I didn't have any expectation that I'd be able to change Mike's perspective on the concept of gender identity, certainly not in a single evening after many beers. And like Mike, I don't believe in all that woo-woo stuff, in karma.

"I'm just tired," Jaime said tensely, already standing.

We clumped ourselves in the hall while our guests put on their things, and I waved to Amy as she walked beside Jaime down the breezeway to the stairs.

Mike stood behind me as we watched them go and massaged my shoulders. I could hear the sound his thumbs made against the cloth of my shirt, a soft scratching hush. And though I strained to hear something more, the coalescing human noises of the whole world from beyond the apartment, all I could hear was Mike. His thumbs, his stomach, his pulse, all that kept him alive behind me.

* * *

Discussion Questions

1. The first half of the story discusses reincarnation. Do you believe in reincarnation or a form of reincarnation? If so, what (*if anything*) is the purpose of reincarnation?
2. The story also talks about soulmates. Do you believe in soulmates or some variation of soulmates?
3. The third part of the story talks about sexual orientation, gender identity, and gender fluidity. Do you believe that sometimes people are born the wrong gender or that people can be both gay and born the wrong gender (i.e., a gay man that was born into a woman's body)?
4. In the cases of questions 1, 2, and 3, what are the scientific, religious, experiential, or value-based constructs we overlay that cause us to come to our own conclusions for each question?
5. In the story, Jaime was born a biological woman, transitioned to a man, but is going to have a baby. Mike questions how to define a man (*or a woman?*) if not by the ability to have children. What would be your answer to this question?

* * *

The House of God

Shannon Frost Greenstein

***

"I don't want to go," the child declared defiantly, and his mother felt her headache ratchet up another notch.

"I know you don't. And I understand why. But we still have to go, so *please* find your other shoe and put them both on."

She was almost entirely successful in masking the strain in her voice, a talent she had developed by necessity over the last several months as she navigated single motherhood with her son and his newly-diagnosed autoimmune condition. But now, there were only twenty more minutes before Mass was scheduled to begin, and they were *still* not in the car, and she was starting to lose her grasp on the threads of her rapidly fraying patience.

"But *why* do we have to?" whined the boy, bottom lip thrust forward, grubby fingers clutching a single shoe. "Why can't we just stay home?"

The woman, fully occupied with brushing cat hair from the child's dress shirt, sighed deeply and paused in her grooming. She wracked her brain for the reason with which her son would be least likely to argue. Unconsciously, her hand rose to hover over the crown of his head; then it dropped suddenly like a weight to fall by her side.

"Because the Bible says blessed are those who dwell in the house of God," she finally responded. "And going to church is how we honor Him."

The woman clutched her fingers into fists as she fought the urge to run her hands through the child's thinning hair. She had always loved how his golden curls felt like silk; it was taking a gargantuan effort to break the habit of caressing his head. She tried not to notice the new bald patch directly behind his ear. Curly blond strands littered the boy's pillowcase every morning. His hairbrush next to the sink now held more hair than his head. The dermatologist said it would eventually become clear if they were dealing with *Alopecia Areata* or *Alopecia Totalis*, and—unfortunately—the passage of time seemed to be suggesting the latter.

"People are gonna stare," the boy muttered after a long silence, tracing the pattern on the bedspread with one finger, refusing to meet his mother's eyes. He brought his own hands to hover near his head, his own fingers clutched into fists, before yanking them back down to his lap as if they were misbehaving.

The pain behind her breastbone took the woman's breath away, and for a moment, she was unable to speak. Her heart ached for her son, and her brain raged at the world, and she was struck with a wave of such impotence that even her steadfast faith in Jesus Christ began to tremble.

"Of course they won't!" she began, one of the many rote recitations of motherhood designed more for the comfort of one's young than to impart any truth whatsoever. Then she stopped, because the truth was she *couldn't* comfort her young—not about this, and not anymore. People *were* going to stare, they had *already* been staring, and there was not a single thing she could say to take this pain away from her child.

Instead, the woman knelt down until she was on the same level as her son and tipped up his chin with her forefinger.

"You are delightful. Losing your hair does not change that, and I feel *bad* for the people who stare, because they aren't *half* as delightful as you."

The boy allowed her to fold him into a hug, even though his own arms remained motionless by his sides.

"Remember... you are special because God made you. He loves you exactly as you are."

She released the child and discreetly wiped away the tears that had formed in her eyes, then handed him the baseball cap, which had been his constant traveling companion since the Alopecia diagnosis.

"And you will *always* belong in the house of God. Now, *please* find your other shoe."

* * *

"The peace of the Lord be with you always."

"And also with you."

The woman clasped the hand of the congregant to her left and murmured a demure, *"Peace be with you."* Then she turned to her right and nudged her son, still seated upon the pew, feet dangling well above the floor.

He stood obediently, avoiding eye contact with the parishioners around him, then dropped to his knees when the time came, behavioral conditioning at its finest.

"Take. Eat. This is my body which is given to you. Do this in remembrance of me."

"Amen."

The boy's mother rose and edged out of the pew, joining the line of congregants assembling for Communion like obedient ducklings. She tugged the boy behind her by the hand, the fingers of his other hand fiddling self-consciously with the patchy hair at his temples.

They meekly approached the altar, the routine eternal and stalwart, ingrained like breathing. Madonna and child, they bowed their heads before the priest, partaking together in the miracle of transubstantiation. The woman prayed to be made worthy of Christ's love; the boy prayed for his hair to grow back.

"Little boys who wear hats in church go to Hell."

The speaker was elderly and stooped; the hat perched on her head like an anachronism was garish, its angle haughty, its veil formal and stiff. She spoke from over his shoulder like a conscience. For a moment, her voice was indistinguishable from the voice he heard in his head when he prayed very hard, something the priest called the *still, quiet voice of God*, and the boy was still dazed when he opened his eyes to glimpse the old woman's sneering face.

"Little boys who wear hats in church go to Hell," she

repeated, then opened her mouth for the sacrament like a baby starling. The stained-glass windows threw their light upon the altar as she chewed, illuminating her face in a rainbow of color, the entire scene seeming to the child like a fever dream from which he could not awake. Struggling to her feet, making the sign of the cross, the old woman treated the child's baseball cap to a final scathing glance, then turned and hobbled back to her pew.

Then it was just the boy and the sanctuary and the silence. And the boy was alone.

* * *

The child was quiet as they drove.

"Are you okay, darling?" his mother questioned more than once, and he would nod, and heavy quiet would descend again.

"That woman just didn't understand," she attempted again, glancing worriedly at her son in the backseat. "She's just old-fashioned. I bet she doesn't even know what Alopecia *is*. You didn't do a single thing wrong."

Finally, as they were turning into the driveway, the boy spoke.

"Momma, if God is choosing to make my hair fall out, then why did Jesus say *God is love?*"

His mother blinked.

"And if He can't make it grow back, why did Jesus say *with God, all things are possible?*"

The car had come to a stop, but the woman sat immobile, staring into the rearview mirror. Recognizing the beat-up Toyota and its motley crew of occupants were dangling over a metaphorical precipice, she rummaged for something to say, searching for an answer she already vaguely understood she would never find.

"Well..." she began, then paused. "He... God *is* love, honey. Your hair... well, it's a disease..."

"Then why won't He stop it?" the child interrupted. "How can He be God if He can't fix it?"

"He *can*," she reassured her son, immediately falling back on a lifetime of faith in the omnipotence of her God. "He just..."

But while faith is a comfort, it's not much of a compendium, and the woman found herself foundering weakly through this declaration. Still waiting for the right words to arrive in a flash of insight, her voice eventually trailed off into nothingness.

"I prayed for Him to take away my Alopecia," said the boy mildly, "and He didn't. Either He doesn't want to, or He can't."

The child unbuckled his seatbelt and opened the door, exiting the car without further comment, while his mother watched his departure with a slack jaw. Taking a minute to gather herself, shaking her head briskly like a dog, the woman finally gathered up her pocketbook and hurried after her son into their modest house.

She found the boy sprawled on the couch, gazing vacantly at a brightly animated Sunday morning cartoon. His dress shoes had been kicked off; his hands were once again curled into fists, held in his lap through sheer force of will.

"Are you okay, angel?" the woman inquired nervously—though why she should be nervous around her own *son* was still not entirely clear.

After a beat, he glanced up to meet her eyes, staring straight through her skull and then into her soul. The woman took a quick step backward, heat rising through her sternum like magma.

"I don't think I want to go to church next week," the boy remarked. Then, returning his eyes to the television, he casually swept the cap from his head.

* * *

Discussion Questions

1. If you were the mother in this story, how would you answer the boy's questions about God allowing his sickness and hair loss?
2. Epicurus argued as part of his "problem of evil" that God cannot be both (1) all-powerful, (2) all-knowing, and (3) all-good because evil (like children's diseases) exists in the world, and therefore, there is no God. This is, essentially, the argument the boy is making. Assuming you believed in God, what convincing counterarguments (*if any*) could you make?
3. Should the mother in the story make her son go to church regardless of his wishes? If so, what reasons might she have for wanting her son to go to church?
4. Should the mother in the story have said something to the person who told her son, "Little boys who wear hats in church go to Hell?" What would you have done (*or said*) in that situation?
5. What are valid and invalid reasons for a parent to force their child to do something they don't want to do?

* * *

Visions of Midwives

C.S. Griffel

* * *

The heavy groan sounded as though it were being dragged from inside the woman's body involuntarily. Her pregnant belly heaved as guttural sounds enveloped the tiny bedroom. Keery dabbed the sweat from the woman's forehead. The midwife, Luanne, examined the woman to check her dilation. A clock on the mantlepiece ticked away the minutes, piling them into hours.

"Illona, you're doing so well, darling. Your baby's head has engaged, and you're going to really start pushing."

Illona responded with only a nod and "uh-huh."

"Keery, come here, girl," Luanne ordered. Keery obeyed quickly. "Place your hand here. Feel that? That's how you can tell the baby's head is engaged. Illona, on your next contraction, you're going to push." Keery was nearing the end of her apprenticeship, so it was not the first time she had felt a baby's head engaged. Still, she obeyed. Each experience was building

Keery up, readying her for her practice.

The process went quickly. It was Illona's sixth baby. Within a few pushes, the baby's head was completely born.

"One more big push, Illona, and your baby will be born." Illona's contraction hit; she scrunched her face until it looked like a closed fist and pushed. Luanne's hands grabbed ahold of the baby as he was suspended in the space between being born and not yet born. The elderly midwife's eyes rolled back as a vision of the child's destiny encompassed her mind. The moment was over as quickly as it had come. The little boy was born. For the briefest moment, Keery saw that Luanne's features were grim. Before Illona could see her face, she wiped it clean of emotion.

"Is it a boy?" Illona asked, her voice breathy and rough from the effort of getting her child out into the world.

"Yes, it's a boy," was Luanne's dry reply.

Keery looked at the tiny baby. He looked perfect. He balled his little hands into fists and kicked with both his legs. She wondered what Luanne had seen. Keery had not yet experienced the second sight, but she knew she would when her turn came to be the attending midwife.

"Take care of Illona, Keery, while I take care of the mite."

Keery's job now was to wait for Illona's body to complete the process of birth. Soon the placenta would appear. Illona did not know that Luanne had seen her son's future. It was a secret long kept by the midwives of their people. The clock tower in the town square chimed out a quarter past one in the morning. Keery noted that the little boy had not yet cried. Illona noticed too.

"Is he all right?" Illona's voice, roughened from groaning, broke the quiet. Luanne did not respond immediately. "Midwife, is he all right, I say?" At this, Luanne wrapped the boy in the soft blanket his mother had carefully knitted for him. Illona didn't have much in the way of wealth, but each of her babies at least got a new blanket, even if it was knitted from yarn carefully undone from his dad and grandad's old sweaters.

Luanne brought the little man to his mother, only his face visible in the mass of soft yarn, just yellow enough to not be white. The midwife handed the waiting mother her child. The mother's eyes were full of fear and love. She glanced at her baby's face, his closed eyes.

"He never drew the first breath of life," Luanne delivered the words gently, but they struck the mother like a fist to her gut. The woman gathered her baby to her, and a wail like the cold winter wind barreling through the high mountains grew out of the woman's belly and shattered the peaceful calm of deep night.

Keery wondered what had happened. She had seen the boy born. He had been kicking and balling up his tiny fists. She knew he had been alive. Confused, Keery glanced at the senior midwife. Luanne's face was a mask of stoic resolve. It was not the time or place to ask questions.

Upon hearing her mournful wail, Illona's husband rushed into the room. He climbed into the bed with his distraught wife and drew her and the baby to himself. He murmured into her ear that he loved her, would always love her, but he did not tell her to be quiet or that it would be okay. He simply allowed her to pour out her grief. Uncaring that they had an audience, the husband held his distraught wife, lest the pain take her away with her child.

Keery helped Luanne gather their things quickly. It was best at this point to leave the grieving family to their pain. It would be the father's job to care for the wee body now. Before they left, the father said, "Your payment is on the mantel, good wife." It was ill luck, even under the circumstances, to leave the midwife unpaid.

As they walked through the damp cold of the night, Keery struggled to put her question into words. What had happened to the child? She alone knew that the midwife had lied. That baby was alive when it was born.

"Luanne..." Keery began. Luanne anticipated the question.

"Child, you will understand when you birth your first baby. You will know when you see what the future has in store. That child was destined for great misery. 'Twas a mercy I done. It is a burden we midwives carry, the purpose of our gift." Her words were sharp and final. Keery knew she would answer no more questions. They parted company near the town square, Luanne to her snug, well-appointed home, Keery to the hovel where she still lived with her parents.

Keery did not sleep that night. She kept thinking of the tiny, perfect arms and legs, unused to the immense space outside the womb, making small, jerking movements, feeling for the boundaries of its new life.

The waning summer brought with it many births. The cold nights of December—all the harvest work done and winter settling in—brought with it many conceptions. Husbands, no longer exhausted from the hard labor of spring, summer, and fall, more frequently sought the affections of their wives.

August was the midwives' busiest month. It also brought an end to Keery's apprenticeship. "There are too many babies coming for me to hold yer hand any longer," Luanna told her as July closed. "We'll place you with the younger mothers who've already had a babe or two." These tended to be the easiest births. The mothers were young enough that the risk of complication was low but had already proven their ability to birth healthy babies.

Keery was summoned for her first birth on August 5th at one in the morning. It was, of course, a full moon. Luanne's errand girl, Peony, rapped loudly on the door, waking Keery and her parents. Keery would not be able to move into her own home until she had earned enough from attending births to purchase one. Her vocation as midwife meant that she would never have a husband. She did not mourn this fact. She had seen many women, married in the rush of youth's lusts, walk an unhappy path when passions cooled. She had also seen young couples wed soberly and advisedly and remain in love their whole lives. Her chances, she supposed, were as good as any to go either way. She simply knew that it was not her destiny to wed. It was part of the midwife's second sight.

"Mildred Connor has gone into labor and needs attendance," Peony said urgently. "Mistress Luanne is attending Morgrid's birth and cannot leave. It's not going well. She sent me to fetch you. She says you must attend Mildred on your own."

Keery nodded and grabbed her midwifery satchel. It had

been a gift from the Midwives' Guild and still smelled and creaked like brand-new leather. "Tell Mistress Luanne I'm on my way." Peony scurried quickly into the darkness.

The walk to the Connor's home was about twenty minutes. Mildred's husband answered the door with a look of relief on his face. "It's going quickly," he said. Keery nodded in response and followed him to the back room where Mildred lay upon the bed, knees tucked back as far as they would go, sweat dripping gently down her forehead. As Keery walked in, Mildred was gripped with a contraction that made her push with all her might. Before Keery could reach her, Mildred's body reflexively pushed out a baby girl. Keery moved to check the baby was all right while Mildred took deep breaths, an automatic response to normalize her breathing. When Keery's hands touched the baby, she received no second sight. This child's destiny remained in the realm of the unknown and the unknowable. It happened often enough that a baby was born before a midwife could arrive, especially with healthy babies. It is only in the moment when the child is suspended between being born and not yet born, when the head has emerged, that midwives receive the sight. Frankly, Keery was relieved. The burden of knowing another person's destiny was frightening, and she was glad to put it off, if even for one more day.

Keery checked over the baby, who showed every sign of being quite healthy. After cleaning the baby, Keery handed her over to her mother, who cooed over her beautiful child in the way just birthed mothers do. "Hello, my darling," she purred into the child's ear, "aren't you pretty?" Mildred rained kisses upon the head of fine, raven black hair. Keery waited with

Mildred until her placenta was born, checking that all was well. When mother, child, and happy family were well settled, she slipped into the bright midday sun, pleased with herself.

Coins jingled merrily in Keery's little purse as she strode through the village on her way home. It wasn't until Peony crossed her path that she noted the somber air of the village. "Peony," she called, "how is Morgrid? Did her child fair well?" Morgrid and her husband had been childless for the first twenty-three years of their marriage. The couple had long since given up hope of ever having a child when Morgrid found she was finally pregnant at forty-two.

The child looked up at Keery, shaking her head, "No," she said. "Morgrid and her babe died."

It was common for there to be complications in birth for first-time mothers in their thirties or forties. Keery was saddened but not shocked at the outcome. This, too, was a part of midwifery, dealing with the loss of mothers in birth. The midwives did all they could to shepherd mother and baby safely through the process, but sometimes, there was nothing they could do. Death was fated.

It was three weeks later when Keery was summoned once again to attend the birth of a young, fourth-time mother. When Keery arrived, the woman's husband answered the door, drunk. "She's in there," the man said as he pointed to a room on the west side of the house, his stance unsteady. Three young children huddled together in a corner. The eldest sister, no more than eight, sat in between two little boys, looking to be about five and three years old, respectively. The sister's arms were protectively draped over the shoulders of her little brothers. She had a hardened look in her eye, something sad to see in one so young. The little girl made eye contact with Keery, and a little smile crossed the child's lips, a welcome for the young midwife. A groan came from the westward room, and the child's eyes darted back to her father as he shouted, "Quit yer yowlin! It's giving me a headache!" Hardness replaced the brief smile in the child's eyes.

"Why don't you step outside, sir, where your wife's cries won't bother you. She'll be fine now that I'm here. It looks like your girl there can look well after her brothers." The man nodded, stumbled out the door, and headed for the pub, Keery was sure. He looked like he had once been handsome, but drink and misery had twisted him into an ugly facsimile of his younger self.

The woman in the bed clung to the headboard rails like a drowning person might cling to driftwood in a raging river. Unlike her husband, prettiness still lingered on this woman's face. Love for her children kept her from total despair.

"You're Agnes, aren't you?" Keery inquired. The woman nodded in reply. "I'm Keery, the midwife. I want you to take some deep breaths." Agnes obeyed and breathed in deeply through her nose. Predictably, Agnes's labor went quickly. She seemed to relax with her husband gone and a midwife present.

No more than thirty minutes after Keery's arrival, the baby's head emerged from the birth canal. Keery placed her hands on the tiny head to support the child as its mother completed the birthing process. When the vision overtook her, the pain was so intense Keery thought she would explode into dust, down to the very last molecule. The sensation lasted only a moment, but within it, Keery felt what seemed an eternity pass. She knew now what Luanne had told her about. She knew this child would experience intense suffering. Yet, as she looked at the tiny, beautiful little girl, now fully born, she knew she could not do what Luanne had done. Keery didn't know if this meant she was cowardly or courageous. She only knew she could not extinguish the light of life burning in the milky blue eyes now blinking up at her.

Keery handed the child to her mother. "A lovely little girl," she said. And like all mothers, Agnes drew the child to herself, murmuring and cooing.

"Margery," Keery heard Agnes whisper. Whatever else may come in this child's life, she was loved and content in this moment with this mother.

Misery did come to the child. When Margery was just three years old, Agnes came to a sad end. A merchant in the marketplace allowed his eyes to linger upon her too long. Her husband, in a drunken and jealous rage, beat her to death, and he was hung the next morning, leaving their four children orphans. No one could afford to take in four children, and they were all separated. Within a few months, the families that had taken in the children woke to find their beds empty. The eldest sister had come in the night for her siblings, unwilling to be apart. What became of them after that, no one in the village knew. Keery surmised the child had gone to the city and taken up prostitution to keep her siblings under a roof and fed. There was appetite enough in the big city, even for very young girls, to keep body and soul together for the little orphans. Keery wondered if she was wrong not to have released Margery from this fate.

Most of Keery's visions portended a mixture of pain, sorrow, joy, and peace. All human lives have some of everything. Of course, there were lives that held more or less joy, more or less pain than others, but she had not yet again felt the pain that had been foretold for Margery. Keery, carefully saving every coin, now lived in a small cottage of her own. It was not ostentatious. In fact, it was small and lacked any luxury, but it was tidy and her own. Keery was now a well-loved midwife, popular with young mothers.

Keery awoke naturally in her own bed for the first time in three days. She had just overseen a first-time mother, and the labor had been slow. Even so, baby was well born, and mother was resting in the glow of new motherhood and the love of a proud husband. She looked at the clock on her mantelpiece. It read 10:00 a.m. Keery felt positively indulgent. She made herself a trencher of cheese and bread and poured a large glass of ale. Tucking in, she enjoyed a leisurely meal by the fire. No knock at the door disturbed her while she swept and dusted her little cottage. She even made it to evening mass. It wasn't until four the next morning that a knock disturbed her rest. Birgitta Hoskin was in labor. She and her husband, Tobias, lived in the manse, the largest home in town. Tobias was a merchant. Keery was lucky to have been chosen to be Birgitta's midwife. The fussy young mother required a lot of attention, which meant Keery was called to the manse for frequent visits. Each visit added more coins to her meager stash. Keery was not greedy by any means, yet she dreamed of delicate curtains adorning her little kitchen window, softening the glow of streaming sunlight.

Birgitta was buxom and well-built for childbearing. Though it was her first baby, her labor was rapid. Her body just seemed to know exactly what to do. It was ready to send baby number one into the world and prepare itself for birthing the next nine that would surely come. Birgitta's baby was crowning within an hour. When her hands touched the blood-stained head of the child, Keery felt something she had never felt before. The terror of a thousand souls ran through her in one split second. Another push from Birgitta and the child was born, and Keery's vision gone. The child would not suffer, she knew, but would cause great suffering. It was a boy lying limply in her hands with the umbilical cord wrapped around his neck. Keery's throat tightened. What should she do? The child had not yet drawn breath. She could let him expire. She could save many from suffering, were her vision to be trusted. It would be easy to say he had been born dead. He had the cord wrapped around his neck. Birgitta was anxiously peering at the midwife and baby through her spread knees.

"Is he all right?" Birgitta asked. Keery looked up at the question and saw in the mother's eyes fear and love for her baby. She looked back down at the limp body, bluish around the lips. He was a perfect baby otherwise. Sweet, like all newborn babies. Without further thought, Keery loosened the cord and coaxed breath into the baby's lungs. Soon, he let out a mighty wail. Keery handed him over to his waiting mother. Stoically, Keery finished the rest of her duties, waiting for the placenta, cleaning and clearing things away, and packing her bag. She left a happy mother with a nursing child as she slipped out of the manse.

Once again, Keery was plagued by the fear that she had done the wrong thing by letting a child live. When she arrived home, she did not unpack her things for her customary cleaning. Instead, she knelt before the little altar in her living room. The statue of the Virgin Mother, wearing robes of robin's egg blue and a gilt crown, had been her one indulgence. It had made a deep gouge in her savings. She prayed to it now, her heart pouring out her fears before the saintly young mother depicted in wood. Was she wrong to allow such suffering into the world if she could stop it? Was Luanne right? Was the purpose of the gift of sight for snuffing out suffering? She looked up at the statue, its beatific eyes staring perpetually up to the heavens. She would get no answer here. Keery looked at her hands. They had helped usher many lives into the world already. She wouldn't use them to usher it out. Perhaps she would answer for it one day. She prayed the virginal lady would speak up for her when the time came. A knock at the door caught her attention. She sighed and stood. It was Peony. "Astrid's water broke," the young woman told her.

"Tell her I'll be right there."

* * *

Discussion Questions

1. Would you be willing to work as a midwife if it meant seeing the future of the child being born?
2. Should any baby be put to death under any foreseeable future? Is there any situation where killing the newborn is the right choice?
3. In the story, Keery hesitates in her decision to allow the birth of a child who will live to cause misery for others. More so than when she decided to allow a child to be born into experiencing a lifetime of misery. Do you agree with this distinction?
4. Would it be better to tell the parents of the child's future so they could choose whether the child lives or dies? What are the pros and cons of this approach?
5. What, if anything, is a practical distinction between killing a child in the story and terminating a pregnancy in modern society when a severe genetic defect is found?

* * *

Playing God

Ilan Herman

* * *

After Jack was abducted by the alien spaceship, and after the round vessel had vanished into the Milky Way, he found himself walking down a tubular corridor with white vibrating walls, escorted by a sinuous blonde who smiled graciously and said her name was Minna. She was tall and well endowed, with sparkling blue eyes, but Jack knew she was a hologram. He also knew that he was supposed to be utterly freaked out by the abduction, but he wasn't and attributed his calm to a narcotic administered by the aliens. Jack felt like his normal self.

Minna stopped walking and touched the vibrating walls. They parted to show an oval room glowing in soft purple. A brown armchair centered the room. The walls were covered with TV screens showing people in distress.

Jack stood in the doorway. "What's this? I don't like it."

Minna smiled widely. "Please sit in the chair."

Jack took a step back. "No way."

Minna held his hand and purred. "No harm will come to you."

She walked toward the chair, Jack in tow, his fingers sliding in and out of her warm palm. The TV screens vanished. The walls pulsated sensually in purple and pink.

Minna gestured to the armchair as if she was a car model at a convention. "Please sit. I promise the chair will not bite you."

Jack sat in the chair. The soft fabric, like liquid silk, curved in a warm embrace. He placed his arms on the wide armrests; they nestled his arms in warm yet firm liquid as if he was floating in a heavily salted sea. The air smelled of roses. Ocean waves rumbled from afar; parrots chirped in a rainforest. His back and shoulders relaxed like after a thorough deep tissue massage. The chair hummed with vibrations that soothed his neck and buttocks.

"Feels nice," Jack said.

Minna laughed. "You like the chair?"

"I do."

"Good," chirped the Nordic queen. "Now you can be god."

"What?"

The multitude of TV screens showing people in distress returned to broadcast from the walls. Minna smiled and pointed to the screens. "You can help them. You can be their god."

Jack nervously tried to sit up in the armchair, but was coddled by soft yet powerful and invisible tentacles that held him like a yearning lover. He sank back into the chair and sighed, "I don't know what you're talking about."

"Help them." Minna pointed to the screens. Her bright smile had faded.

Jack looked up at one of the screens. Bearded men wearing white gowns were throwing stones at a young woman no older than sixteen.

"What are they doing?" he yelled.

"They are trying to kill her," Minna said. "She gave her virginity to the wrong man."

Jack frowned. "How do they know what's good for her?"

Minna shrugged, her blue eyes filled with sadness. "They do not. Do you want to stop them from hurting the woman?"

"Yes," he hissed and narrowed his eyes.

Minna pointed to the screen. "Tell them to stop."

Jack yelled, "Stop!"

One man about to cast a stone froze in his tracks. Then he started shouting and waving his arms and then lunged at another man who'd thrown a rock at the weeping woman who cowered on the ground, blood trickling from her brow, face shielded by her arms. Several men then attacked the man who attacked the man who threw the rock. A brawl ensued, with knives and heavy clubs. The woman scurried off and found shelter in a brick hut on the village outskirts. The men continued fighting until an elder with a long white beard and a wide gown rushed over, waved his arms, and roared, "Cease your fighting."

Four men lay dead, and seven more, bleeding and unconscious. All were quickly carried into brick huts by their family members.

* * *

Minna smiled and clapped. "You stopped them from killing the woman."

"Why are you happy?" Jack cried. "Four men died."

"But the woman lived."

"But at what cost?"

Minna smiled nervously. "I do not know. You are their god."

Jack wrestled the chair and tried to escape the liquid armrests. "Screw this god crap. I don't want to do this." He struggled mightily, but the warm tentacles held him firmly in the chair.

"Get me out of here," he yelled.

Minna flashed her sunny smile. "I do not know how to do that."

"What do you mean? You promised the chair wouldn't bite. I got news for you, lady, it bites. Now get me out of here."

"You are their god," Minna said, voice fading while her image vanished and was replaced by a chubby bald man with a well-groomed silver beard and thick spectacles.

"What is your problem?" the man asked sternly in a clipped German accent.

"Who are you?" Jack asked.

"I am Siegfried, your psychoanalyst. Why are you afraid of being god?"

"Why?" Jack pointed to the screen. "Look what I did? I can't be god."

Siegfried's hand swerved like a gentle wave. "Even god makes mistakes. You will need practice. Go back to your childhood. Did your mother breastfeed you?"

"This is bullshit," Jack yelled and struggled with the invisible tentacles that continued to shackle him to the armchair. "I'm not talking to any more holograms. Get me a real person to talk to, or I'm staying in this chair and starving myself to death."

The TV screens showing distress vanished from the walls. Siegfried paced the room, hands clasped on the small of his back. "Denying yourself sustenance is clear proof that you want to punish your father for sleeping with your mother." He stopped pacing and frowned at Jack. "Why do you hate your father?"

"I don't hate my father," Jack yelled, a shudder of panic in his voice.

"Then you must eat," said the therapist and snapped his fingers.

A red tray with Jack's favorite meal—a rack of ribs smothered with barbeque sauce and mashed potatoes and coleslaw—appeared from thin air, floated toward him, and landed softly in his lap. Steam rose from the food and tingled his nose with a fresh, meaty aroma that had him salivating. Confused and angry, Jack nonetheless took a bite. The invisible tentacles stretched just enough for him to do so. The delicious meat melted in his mouth. The mashed potatoes were cooked with perfect portions of butter and garlic; the coleslaw was thick and juicy.

The human ignored the hologram of the German therapist and devoured the food. When he finished, the tray floated away. The screens returned. Siegfried gestured toward them with his chin and said, "It is easier to be god on a full stomach."

* * *

On one of the screens, Jack saw a black man slumped against a dumpster in a dark alley. He wore a torn pair of jeans and a stained white T-shirt, and his braided hair was thick with dusty smog. The man, hands shaking, reached into his underpants and pulled out a syringe, a spoon, and a bag of white rocks. He placed a rock in the spoon, struck a lighter, and let the flame heat the bottom of the spoon. The rock melted in a bubbly hiss. The man sucked the liquid into the syringe. He flicked a finger against his arm and found a vein. Hands shaking, he aimed the syringe and was about to puncture his skin when Jack whispered, "Stop."

The disheveled man looked up and around, searching for the voice. He put the syringe on the ground. His hands no longer shook, and the ambivalence in his dark eyes was replaced by sadness. Tears streamed down the man's wrinkled cheeks. He placed his face in his palms and wept for a long time. Then he stood up. He left the syringe and drugs on the ground next to the dumpster and staggered out of the alley.

Siegfried clapped his chubby hands and exclaimed, "He will never do heroin again. He has heard the word of god."

"He wasn't doing heroin. He was doing crack, and stop being so happy. The man has no money or job, probably sleeps on the streets," Jack said with a frown, though he was also satisfied that he was able to stir the junky toward sobriety, however tentative. Then he shook his head with dismay: the aliens were sucking him into their sordid plan, plying him with an attractive woman, a magical armchair, and delicious food. He was a dog in training, doing tricks for treats. Why were they doing that to him?

Jack narrowed his eyes at the analyst hologram. "I see what you're trying to do. Forget about it. I don't want to play god." He tried to cross his arms over his chest, but the soft tentacles kept his arms anchored to the chair.

Siegfried pursed his lips. "You will play god, and you will like it."

"Screw you," Jack said. "I wanna go home. Now beat it and send someone real I can talk to." He shut his eyes for several moments.

When he opened his eyes, Siegfried was gone, replaced by a flame much like one burning a candlewick. The flame, about six feet away, circled him slowly and silently.

"Who are you?" Jack asked.

"I am Koy, from planet Zoomar," the flame said in a high-pitched voice. "This is how I look. I am not a hologram."

"Cool," said Jack. "I believe you. You sound like a nice alien, but do something about your voice. It's squeaky. And then get me out of this chair."

"I will release you," Koy said in a soft baritone, "but I would like to convince you to use the armchair and help us."

The tentacles let go of Jack's arms. He stood up and paced the room. "One minute, I'm watching Seinfeld in my living room, the next I'm in a spaceship. I don't have a problem with that, but," he stopped pacing and frowned at the flame, "some would call what you did *kidnapping*."

"I apologize," Koy said, voice ringing with sincerity, "but

we need your help."

Jack started pacing again. "How can I, a puny human, help you, a superior extraterrestrial?"

The flame shimmered for a moment and then said, "We, the scientists of Zoomar, do not know how to fix mankind."

"Why do you care about mankind? We're pretty hopeless."

"We created you," Koy said slowly, deep sadness in his voice.

Jack stopped pacing. "Say what?"

Koy explained that planet earth was used as a Petri dish to sprout the seeds of life planted by Zoomarian scientists, a genetically engineered experiment that had gone wrong. "Man has become a vicious creature who kills and consumes without care. We need humans to change, to evolve, or we will have no choice but to suspend the experiment. We dread this outcome with every fiber of our enlightenment, but we have lost control. Nothing we do changes human nature." Koy's voice shook with frustration.

"Easy does it, buddy," Jack said. "There's no crying in genetic engineering."

The flame expanded. "What you just said is a perfect example of my inability to understand humans. What you just said makes no sense at all."

"Sure it does," the human said. "It's a take on Tom Hanks saying, 'There's no crying in baseball.' That's from the movie *A League of Their Own*."

If the flame had fists it could clench and raise to the heavens, it would surely do so while cussing loudly. Instead,

Koy's voice cracked with emotion. "That is why we need you and others like you, smart human beings who understand the subtlety and nuance of culture and language—"

"You have other people you talk to?" Jack cut in and pointed to the armchair. "Others you have sit in chairs and watch videos?"

"Yes. One more."

"And you ask that person to play god?"

"Yes. Her name is Matilda. She is very insightful and helpful." The flame shimmered. "She knows how to curb the violence."

"And if I say I don't wanna be god, will you let me go?"

"Of course," Koy said. "What good would it serve us to keep you against your will?"

Jack pointed to the armchair. "If I sit in the chair now, can I get up anytime I want?"

"Yes," the exasperated flame whispered.

Jack sat in the brown armchair and was surrounded by warm comfort. Then he stood up. The tentacles didn't stop him. Deep in thought, he paced the room while the flame silently looked on.

"Why didn't you show up first instead of Minna or that silly therapist?" Jack asked.

"You are a man, so we wanted to entice you with an attractive woman, and when that failed, we opted for an authoritative figure."

Jack chuckled. "Minna was hot, but that Freud impersonator was whacky, not convincing at all."

A sigh fluttered the flame. "I trust that you now see that

we have lost our capacity to understand what human beings like and want, why they behave the way they do."

Jack shrugged. "Welcome to parenthood. You raise a kid, think you know them, then they turn thirteen, and it's like you have no idea who they are. Sad but true."

Silent camaraderie ensued for a moment, and then Koy said, "Would you like to meet Matilda?" A proud parent crept into his voice. "She is a wonderful emotional translator."

Jack laughed. "Emotional translator? Can we get a little more cumbersome? Sure, I'll be happy to meet Matilda."

* * *

Flame and man left the oval room and proceeded down the white corridor with the liquid walls until the flame stopped. The walls parted to show a room much like the one they'd left, except the walls were dark green. The room was centered by a lime-green armchair. A diminutive woman sat in the chair. About seventy years old, white hair well-groomed and puffed up with hairspray, she had a wide forehead plowed with wrinkles, a hooknose, thin lips dabbed with red lipstick, and blue eyes that twinkled with a child's curiosity. Her bony left forefinger, manicured and stained with pink nail polish, pointed rapidly from one screen to the next.

"No, you cannot do this," she said to one screen, and then, "Yes. Do it," to the next. She spoke with a British accent, which American viewers, Jack included, found dignified and colorful when watching PBS Mystery Theatre. Because she worked swiftly, the people in distress showing on the screens were quickly replaced by more anguished people. She ignored Jack and Koy, who stood in the doorway. They watched in silence while the older woman worked and seldom took more than a few seconds to decide.

Matilda then snapped her fingers. The screens vanished into the walls. She reached into the purse, propped against the armchair, and took out a pack of Rothman's. She lit one and then smiled at the guests. "Hello, Koy. And who might be the dashing young man you've brought to meet me?"

"Jack Straw," said Jack and saluted casually.

Matilda smiled. "How old are you, and what do you do for a living?"

"Forty-two, Madam, and I'm a software engineer."

Her eyes widened as she formed her lips in a circle. "Quite the title. Are you married, and do you have children?"

"No on both counts. I guess I have intimacy issues."

Matilda had a deep laugh riddled with decades of smoking. "Some solitary people are more loving than ones with mates and children. Not all is what it seems."

"You should know," Jack said and pointed to the walls. "How long you been doing this?"

"Six months."

Jack whistled. "How do you last? So much misery and craziness."

"Quite simple," said the crusty dame. "I have three daughters and one son, and eleven grandchildren and four great-grandchildren. I'm trying to save them." Then Matilda looked at Koy's flame and asked, "Why did you choose him?"

The flame shimmered. "He thinks very quickly."

"Maybe he does, but is he compassionate?"

"When he finds spiders in his apartment, he traps them

in a cup and releases them in his backyard. He takes care to step over a column of ants. Even though he doesn't have children, he donates money to foundations that help orphans in Africa."

"How do you know all that?" Jack cried. "How long have you been spying on me?"

"We are in search of emotional translators," Koy said. "We mean no disrespect to your privacy. We make sure to never watch when you are taking a shower or using the bathroom, and we empathically cease our surveillance when you entertain female company."

Jack frowned. "Thanks a lot. You guys are a pushy bunch of aliens."

The flame contracted. "We offer our sincere apology. We mean no harm."

"The road to hell is paved with good intentions," said Jack. "I think your failed experiment proves that."

Matilda put out her cigarette in a floating ashtray and chuckled. "The experiment isn't a failure yet, though it is teetering over the abyss. Koy and his fellow scientists can be as ambivalent and insensitive as humans, but they have no malice. Have you considered why you want to play god?"

"I'm not sure that I do," Jack said. "I saved a woman from being stoned, but then four men got killed. I don't think I'm good at playing god. Besides, I don't have the temperament. I'll probably start hating people real quick."

Matilda nodded. "Legitimate concerns no one but you can consider. Perhaps a few days as a trial period will help you decide?"

"Maybe," Jack said and shrugged. "At least the food here

is good."

Matilda laughed. "That it is." Then she narrowed her blue eyes. "You should try out. After all, what could be nobler than saving the human race?"

"But what if I keep screwing up?"

Matilda smiled. "Playing god is like riding a bike. You'll fall and scrape your knee, but then you'll get up, dust yourself off, and get back on the bike. You get better at it. Now, if you'll excuse me, I must get back to work. Come visit with me tomorrow if you decide to stay. I like you." Matilda snapped her fingers. The screens came alive on the walls.

Jack and Koy left the green room that was swallowed by the white walls. Then Koy said, "If you wish, you can try working an hour or two a day, so as not to be overwhelmed. That way, you can maintain your life on earth. The molecular transport is quick and harmless."

"I like that option," Jack said, perhaps somewhat empowered to try to save humanity.

They arrived at the room with the brown armchair. Jack sat in the chair, stretched his legs, and said, "Comfy." Then he looked at Koy's flame. "How about one screen at a time instead of a whole bunch?"

"Of course," said the alien scientist, voice filled with gratitude.

Jack shook his head. "You guys are clueless about humans. You got in way over your head."

"Zoomarians do not have heads," Koy said.

Jack rolled his eyes. "It's a figure of speech," and then he waved his right arm. "Never mind. Come back in an hour."

The walls parted to allow the flame to leave the room. Jack rubbed his palms, heart beating quickly with nerves. He took a deep breath and looked up at the screen:

* * *

Raising clouds of dust, a jeep rumbles across the Kenyan savannah. The driver is a young black man. Two white men dressed in khaki and wielding hunting rifles sit in the back.

"Over there," one of them shouts and points to the herd of elephants. He has a thin mustache and icy-blue eyes. The jeep veers toward the large beasts. The elephants see the jeep and start to run, but the jeep gains on the herd. The man with the thin mustache places the rifle against his shoulder and shouts, "I'm getting the big one on the left."

The herd's rumble grows louder. Warning cries trumpet from their trunks. The jeep is upon the large elephant leading the herd, his tusks long and sharp. The man shuts his left eye and aims. His finger caresses the trigger. Then his arms start to shake. The bewildered look in his blue eyes overtakes the steely confidence.

"Shoot the bloody thing," the other man yells. "What are you waiting for?"

The hunter slowly shakes his head. "I can't."

"What do you mean you can't, you bastard? We paid fifty grand to shoot an elephant."

The hunter with the thin mustache raises his rifle to the sky and lets go with a round that sails over the herd. The second hunter aims his rifle at the large elephant but then points his rifle at the ground and unloads his bullets. The herd moves on. The hunters remain seated in the back of the jeep, arms dangling to their sides.

"What happened?" the blue-eyed one mutters.

"Hell, if I know," the other hunter says, "but suddenly, I don't want to kill an elephant."

The man with the thin mustache shakes his head. "Neither do I. Let's go back to camp and get drunk."

Sitting in his brown armchair in the oval room pulsating in soft purple, Jack raised his arms in triumph and cried, "I saved an elephant."

Koy, now a sky-blue oval, floated in through the walls. "I am very happy, and I sense you are happy too."

"Yup."

"So you will come back and help us make the world a better place?"

Jack laughed. "Well, since you put it that way, I don't have a choice, do I?"

"I do not know. Do you?"

"Never mind, you're hopeless," Jack said and stood up. "See you tomorrow, same place, same time."

* * *

Discussion Questions

1. If you were given the opportunity to save humanity, like Jack, would you accept the offer?
2. If you were selected, how would you focus your efforts to improve humanity? For example, would you, as Jack, use short commands? Is there an area of humanity you would focus your attention on?
3. If you were given the chance to try to help people and save humanity, would it be immoral to decline, or would a moral person be required to accept the offer?
4. If you were the Zoomarians, what would be the traits of the person you would select to play god? Is there a particular profile, or series of questions, you would use to screen the perfect applicant?
5. What do you think are the long-term effects on the person playing god? Do you think a person could assist the Zoomarians for years or decades?

* * *

And Joy Shall Overtake Us as a Flood

Daniel James Peterson

* * *

A few days after the accident, a nurse removes the bandages from my face and hands me a mirror. A troll stares back at me while the nurse says something about cosmetic surgery. When I don't respond, he leaves me alone to stare at myself. My face aches in the places where shards of rock or glass worked their way under my skin, the pain doubling as I poke and prod the tiny mounds of flesh. I trace my index finger from one intersection where fresh scars meet age lines to the next. My face is misshapen, unrecognizable; yet, inexplicably, I know this monster. I run a hand across my clean-shaven head and watch the creature do the same, never breaking eye contact.

"It was me," I think. "All along, it was me."

I reach for a cigarette to calm my racing heart.

* * *

When the call comes, I'm in the shower. It's been several

weeks since the accident, long enough for the mechanic to fix my car better than the doctors fixed my body. Not so long, though, that my showers aren't punctuated with plinks as pieces of gravel and translucent plastic work their way free from my skin and fall with the water to the tiled floor. I haven't left my house since I got home from the hospital. My days have been a steady stream of reality TV and painkillers. But I force myself to shower daily, even though twisting to wash my body leaves me sore. I know something important is coming, something I need to be ready for when it comes, even if it means ten minutes a day of coughing from shower steam hitting my recuperating lungs.

I notice the voicemail once I'm back in my weathered recliner. My phone blinks an angry red, like it blames me for missing the call. I sigh and tell it to play the message, expecting another diatribe from Brianna. I didn't tell her about the accident until I'd been home from the hospital for a week. She was furious, screaming at me while choking back tears.

"Reza, why did you wait so long to call me? Why didn't you call me in the hospital?" she asked, none of the characteristic bitterness staining her voice. For the first time in over a decade, I wondered if there was something there I could salvage, if there was some response to her question I could give that would pull us back into each other's orbit.

"It didn't really occur to me," I lied.

When the bitterness returned to her voice, its edge was keen. "What if you had died? Was I supposed to learn about the accident from your obituary?"

"When I die, there won't be an obituary. Not in any paper

you'd read, anyway." She yelled, and we fought, and finally, she hung up the phone in anger only to call back the next day and tell me, her voice carefully restrained, that she was here for me if I needed anything. I thanked her, hoping that was all. But she continued, emphasizing that it was healthy for people who'd experienced traumatic events to talk through their feelings, and that different people dealt with trauma in different ways, and...

And I knew, as the restraint drained from her tone, that her phone call wasn't about me. It was about her.

It was always about her.

That conversation didn't resolve anything, but that didn't stop her from calling. After over a week of listening to her play therapist over my protestations that I didn't care about my own death, I just stopped answering my phone, letting my inbox bloat with message after message from her. But this voicemail isn't from Brianna.

"Good afternoon, Mr. Hilbert." The woman's voice is authoritative, taking compliance for granted. "My name is Perez, with the Southeastern Division of the U.S. Time Travel Department in Atlanta. We have important business to discuss. When you can, please contact me at—" Her message cuts off as I tell my phone to dial her callback number. Perez picks up on the second ring.

* * *

After arriving at USTTD the next day, I'm put through several hours of physical and mental evaluations I'm sure I just barely pass. I listen to an endless set of rules and sign half a dozen nondisclosure and compliance agreements.

Finally, I'm ushered into the office of Perez—the only

first name she ever offers me is "Agent"—a tall, tan woman with a gray suit and a painfully tight black ponytail.

"Thank you for coming," Perez begins, giving me a wide, warm smile that clashes with her perfunctory tone. She's trying to put me at ease, but her mission is doomed from the start; there's too much at stake for me to let my guard down around her. I focus on my breathing and my heartbeat, willing them into something resembling normalcy.

"I'm sure you're wondering why you're here," she says.

I choose my words carefully. "Years and years ago, I met someone who looked just like I do now. I imagine your call has something to do with that."

Perez nods calmly, as if what I just said was perfectly normal. "That would explain your TAA several weeks ago."

"T-A-A?"

"Temporal anomaly alert. Our agency's priority is searching for kinked, self-intersecting four-dimensional worldtubes that could pose a problem for our universe's spatiotemporal integrity. When our monitors find such a worldtube, they issue a TAA."

My eyes glaze over at her jargon. "I don't understand. Are you calling me kinky?"

Perez rolls her eyes. "Cute," she deadpans. "Let's start by establishing your frame of reference. Tell me what you know about time travel."

I shrug. "Just what's been on the news, I guess. The tech was invented ten years ago, and chrononauts have been visiting the past ever since. I've read a few articles about scientific breakthroughs and policy changes resulting from discoveries uncovered by these trips, though only those with the right security clearance would know the truth, I guess. I also know that, like any big military secret, it's the kind of thing the general public can't know too much about."

"That's close enough to accurate," Perez says. "And it's worth mentioning that there's a lot about time travel even we don't yet understand. But given what we're preparing you to do, you have a right to have some of your questions answered, and I have a pretty good guess as to what the first question you'll ask is."

"Can the past be changed?"

"Bingo. Now, I could give you a long, sophisticated, nuanced answer to this question. If you want, I can bring in one of our scientists to explain why Lewisian coherentism beats paradox and parallel theory. But the bottom line is, we're absolutely certain that it's impossible to change the past in any meaningful way."

My chest burns. "You can't know that."

"I can, and I do. Every new chrononaut believes the same thing, that he'll be the one to change history. It's a thought that excites some and paralyzes others in fear. But we've been doing this for a while, and I can confidently tell you that no one's ever successfully managed it. Unfortunately, some folks who've tried have gotten hurt very badly in the process."

"What do you mean?"

"Let's say you go back in time to stop Abraham Lincoln's assassination. You head toward his box at the theater to warn him about Booth. But you won't succeed because Lincoln was assassinated. So we know you'll fail, but we don't know how.

Maybe the theater's locked, and you can't get in. Maybe you're arrested before you get close to him. Or maybe you have a heart attack and die right before he does. There are a million different ways you could fail to change the past. The harder you try to change it, the more likely you are to be stuck with one of the nasty, painful outcomes for yourself."

I start to laugh sardonically, but it mutates into a coughing fit. Once I regain my composure, I stare at Perez. "You really expect me to believe all those forms I had to sign about following your regulations were just to ensure my own safety?"

"Yes."

"And if I don't?"

Perez shrugs. "Frankly, I don't care what you believe as long as you follow our rules."

"And if I don't?"

Perez reaches into her desk, then stands over me and hands me a pile of paper. "Mr. Hilbert, here are copies of the agreements you signed. Read them over as many times as you need to get straight on this point. If it takes a few months, we can postpone your TDE…"

"No! No, I get it," I say. "No trying to change the past."

Perez looks at me suspiciously. "We're clear about this?"

"Crystal," I say.

"All right. Any other questions?"

"What's a TDE?"

"Temporally displaced encounter," Perez says, then shoos me out of her office.

* * *

The morning of my TDE, Atlanta traffic lives up to its reputation. I smoke half a pack while waiting for green lights. When I arrive at the lab's parking lot, it's 8:07 a.m. Somehow, I still have nearly half an hour to kill. I pull the note from my pocket. It's wrinkled now, and the ink is fading in parts, so I put on my glasses to read the yellow paper with the instructions I wrote to myself.

"Remember!" a very slightly younger me commands.

"First, Amy," it continues, but Amy's name is crossed out and replaced with "Nadia." Nadia had been forty-three when she started her clinic. I panic for a moment, unable to remember where she was when she died, until I see that, further down the page, I've scrawled "Somalia" in capital letters and drawn an arrow to connect it with Nadia's name. What year would it have been when Nadia turned forty-three? I should be able to do the math, but I'm nervous, and my blunt knives can't cut much these days. I used to do calculations like this so quickly.

"Second, Brianna," comes next, but I scratched out Brianna and wrote in Amy. No matter how many years pass, that wound remains wide open. I can't read reminders like "August 11" and "Buy better baby monitor!" if I want to get to the rest of the list, so I skip them and keep reading.

To my chagrin, I realize that I never did figure out what I should tell myself to do about Brianna. Perhaps it would have been best if we'd never met, or if we'd never dated, or if we hadn't stayed out late together that November evening where she drank too much wine, and I said things I couldn't take back, and she kissed me with tears running down her cheeks like she had just discovered that everything she'd ever wanted out of life had been distilled onto my lips. But when I start to ask what we could have done to make things work, whether we could have come back from Amy's death if I hadn't been such an ass or if she hadn't been so stubborn and cold, my many failures interweave into a jumbled knot, and there's no single cut that will let me pull the whole thing apart. So maybe it's better that I just wrote "Brianna." I instinctively reach for another cigarette.

I'm jarred by a knock on my window. It's Perez. I panic as my eyes dart back to the note.

She opens the car door. "Good morning, Mr. Hilbert. You're here early."

I give what I hope is a nonchalant shrug as I shove the note back into my pocket. "Well, I left home early. You know how bad Atlanta traffic can be."

"I do. We're ready whenever you are." I look at the clock. It's already 8:21. I had thought it was earlier. I thought I had more time.

But I have Nadia's and Amy's and Brianna's names and faces and smiles bouncing around in my head, and correcting those failures would be enough.

* * *

The preparation for my TDE at the lab is strange enough that I begin to wonder if this is all just some elaborate practical joke the government likes to play on elderly car crash victims. Techs fit me with a black harness covered in blinking LEDs and too many straps. It makes me feel like I'm in someone's Christmas-themed sex dungeon. After the techs help me get my suit on over the harness, I discreetly triple-check to make sure the note is still in my front pocket.

Once I'm dressed, they put me in a giant glass box they call an ionization chamber. When I ask what it's for, they say it tells the harness what to send through time so that I don't end up sixty years in the past buck-naked or missing my left ear. Then they change the ambient light to some frequency that makes my body vibrate. The joke about dismemberment leaves me nervous, and I'm thinking about all the things that could go wrong as I'm loaded into a van with a bunch of expensive equipment and driven halfway across town because, as the techs remind me, "time travel isn't space travel."

Cherokee Avenue Methodist Church hasn't aged well. The wooded area behind it is dense and untamed, as if the church gave up fighting a battle against nature it knew it couldn't win. The lot is crawling with black-suited government agents who have secured the area for my TDE.

The van pulls into a parking space next to an old dirt footpath into the brush. The techs hop out and begin setting up silvery devices whose function I can only guess at. I see Perez step out of a blue sedan that followed us to the lot, and we lock eyes briefly before one of her underlings swoops in, talking low and fast. I dust myself off and straighten my tie, hoping I look less rumpled than I feel.

One of the black-suited agents ushers me down the path into the trees, placing me in a spot equally hidden from both the park and the church. "This should do," he says, then disappears before his words have finished registering.

I glance around. I expected everything to look smaller. I

haven't been back here in decades, even though I live only a few miles away. This wooded area always felt so big to me when I was a child, a magical forest in the middle of Atlanta's urban sprawl. I'm bigger now, but the trees didn't stop growing just because I wasn't visiting them. I guess we both grew up, leaving behind well-manicured childhoods for the wild neglect of adulthood.

"Are you ready?" Perez startles me out of my reverie, and I wonder how long she's been standing there. A nearby agent staring at his phone is giving her a thumbs up.

I wish I had time for one more cigarette. Instead, I just nod.

"Good," she says and hands me what looks like a vintage hearing aid. "This is the last piece of your outfit. It allows us to communicate with you in real time so we can let you know if there's a problem or help you correct course if you're close to violating our protocols. We'll also send you reminders at the ten-, five-, and one-minute mark before your TDE ends."

I stare back in confusion. "How can you know how long I'll be?"

"All TAAs are of a known, fixed duration. What you're about to do will take place in the past, Mr. Hilbert. It's already happened."

I pause, clearing a dozen thoughts from my head at once, then just nod and wedge the hearing aid in my ear. "Can I respond to you?"

"The harness you're wearing is embedded with sensitive surveillance equipment. If you say something, we'll hear you. Just don't be too obvious talking to us around other people."

"Okay," I say. "I'm ready."

Perez smiles. "Remember what we covered in orientation. If you need anything, just ask. We can pull you back at any time."

I can't tell if her final words are meant to be reassuring or threatening. Regardless of her intent, they ring hollow. There's no way they'd risk changing the past by letting an old man disappear right before a child's eyes, right? But I just reply, "Noted."

Perez gives her agent a thumbs up. He removes what looks like a remote control from his pocket and presses a button. The harness begins to hum, and my torso vibrates softly. Then there's pain, the harness constricting and pulling and yanking until I feel like a rag doll tossed about a raging sea. My face goes hot, then cold, and my head starts to swim as the world around me fades in and out of focus. I fall to my knees, head in my hands.

Suddenly, the harness's scream dies down to a gentle purr, and my body feels like it's mine again.

* * *

Sweating profusely, I pull myself slowly to my feet to take in a shorter and tidier group of trees than the one I was just standing in. My heart jumps into my throat. I hear Perez's voice come in through my earpiece.

"Your trip was a success, Mr. Hilbert. How are you feeling?"

"Fine," I mutter, dizzily pushing myself forward toward the parking lot. There's an ocean of parked cars, and on the far shore, the back entrance to the church's Fellowship Hall. Sitting on the steps, looking bored, is a boy in a black suit and tie. His suit and shoes look brand new, I think, and then catch myself because I remember they are brand new. My mother and father bought me that suit for my grandfather's memorial service when I was six. That service's reception is happening right now, behind the closed doors that tower above little Reza. Beyond those doors are my mother and father and sister and grandmother, all meeting with friends and family, consoling each other and eating finger sandwiches while Reza, who can't stand being hugged by another old person he's never met, has snuck away to sit on the steps behind the church, alone and bored.

It'd be so easy to push past him, to enter the church and see my dead family one last time. But there's something in the kid's eyes, like a fish suffocating on the deck of a boat, that makes it hard to focus on anything else.

He sees me approaching the church when I'm about halfway across the parking lot, then shifts his eyes back to the cars. I'm just another old man to him. I walk up the steps to the Fellowship Hall and stop next to him.

"You're..." I start, and my voice cracks. My chest feels tight, and I start over. "You're Reza Hilbert, right?"

"Yeah," he tells me, looking up and really seeing me for the first time. "What happened to your face?"

"Car crash."

"You look kinda like Grandpa. Are you his brother?"

My mind flails for a bit before I recall my resolution: no trying to remember our conversation from his side, no saying things just to match those memories. I owe more to myself than to a bunch of government agents, and I'll say what I feel like saying as long as it doesn't blow my shot to make things right.

"Yeah," I answer. "I'm his brother. Sorry I didn't make it for the service. How was it?"

Reza shrugs. "Sad. Mom and Dad were sad. And boring. They're talking with a lot of old people."

"Want to get out of here?" I ask him, and he looks up in confusion. "Where would you like to go, Reza? There's a nice park on the other side of those trees. Maybe we can—"

"I'm not supposed to go anywhere with strangers."

"But I'm not a stranger," I point out. "I'm your grandfather's brother. Your parents will be busy with the reception for a while. They won't mind if your great-uncle takes you to the park for a bit."

Reza ponders my argument for a moment. "Okay," he says and leaps to his feet. The kid loves the park.

We take off across the parking lot. After a few awkward, silent seconds, I ask, "What do you want to talk about while we're walking?"

"Tell me a story," he says, more request than command, and I frown. It's too soon for me to tell him about anything that matters—my head's still reeling from the weirdness of talking to my kindergartener self about my long-dead family.

"Here's the deal," I say. "I'll tell you a story at the end of our trip if you tell me three stories first."

Reza considers, and I can't help but smile at him even as my heart pounds in my chest. "Okay," he says. "What kind of story do you want?"

"Maybe something about your grandpa?" I suggest, and

Reza nods.

"Once upon a time, there was a man who was smarter than everyone else. Even Dad says so. His name was Grandpa Farzin, and everybody loved him so much and was really sad when he died."

Flashes of the past burst in my head, fragmented memories of my grandfather and of the twist I know Reza's story is about to take. I have to steady myself against a parked car to catch myself from stumbling as the world spins around me in a moment of lightheaded *déjà vu*.

"But he had an enemy stronger than any enemy ever, and that enemy was Emperor Glorstugg, leader of the Slugrians, and he hated Farzin because when Farzin was a boy, he flew up to the Slugrian home world on golden wings and killed Glorstugg's dad to free all the Slugrian slaves."

I smile and almost laugh. This must be what going crazy feels like because I remember now. I remember, and I want to interrupt Reza, but I know better because he's just getting warmed up.

"So Glorstugg sent his three strongest warriors to Earth to kill Farzin. One was—" Reza pauses for a moment, sizing me up "—a giant cockroach named Cora-Cora. He shoots fire out of his eyes. And one is a giant scorpion named Scorpo. He shoots ice out of his eyes. And the last one..."

I can see the mischievous glint in Reza's eyes and sigh inwardly.

"He's a giant wasp named Waspy-Wasp, and he shoots poison out of his butt!" Reza titters, very proud of himself. I purse my lips and nod.

"Then what?" I ask.

"Oh, Farzin kills them all with a hammer made of light," Reza replies like it's the most obvious thing in the world. "And he goes to the Slugrian home world and smashes all the bad guys there with his hammer, and then he comes home and marries my grandma and lives happily ever after. The end. Did you like my story?"

"I like it very much, but I don't think it's quite accurate."

"Accur-rate?"

"True. It's not true."

"You didn't ask for a true story," Reza responds. "You asked for a story. I gave you a story."

I can't argue. "Well, it was a good one, anyway. Did your mom and dad tell you how your grandpa died?"

"They said his brain got cancer. He was sick for a long time."

"He was. He suffered a lot, and toward the end, he had trouble remembering who you and your mother and your father were, and that made him really sad."

"How do you know that?" Reza asks, and I want to blurt out everything, tell him who he is and who I am and what's going on, spill all the secrets he'll need to know so that he doesn't make all the mistakes I've made.

But I feel the hum of the harness and am stupidly afraid.

It would be so easy to throw out the earpiece and just start telling Reza everything I want to say. But I don't. I'm weak and scared and not ready to make my move yet. And my head hurts.

"I just know," I say. "Like I said, he's my brother."

"Did you get along with Grandpa?" Reza asks.

"Not always," I say. "It's like with you and your sister."

Reza crosses his arms. "We never get along," he says. "But it's her fault. She's really bossy!"

"Big sisters always are," I reply in a voice I hope sounds knowing. "But she loves you."

"Everyone always says that everyone loves you, but I don't know," Reza says. "That doesn't mean they aren't mean sometimes."

"Are you ever mean to the people you love?" I already know the answer.

"I guess," Reza sighs. He's getting bored. Luckily, we've reached the end of the path and are standing at the edge of Grant Park. "Are there any playgrounds here?"

"Yeah," I reply. "And a zoo."

"A zoo!" His eyes light up. "What kind of animals do they have? Do they have tigers? They're my favorite!"

"Yeah, they do. They're my favorite too."

"Let's go there after the playground," he says decisively, and I realize I've just led Reza on. We never make it to the zoo. My headache is growing worse. It's hard to keep all of these lies straight—the lies I've told, and the lies I will tell. "Hey, Reza, why don't you tell me your second story?"

"Okay," Reza says, but then he sees a playground, and nothing else matters. I can hear him begin the story as he runs ahead, but his voice is soft, and I can't keep up with him, so all I get is "Once upon a time..." before he's scampering up a plastic climbing wall, dirtying his brand-new suit.

He doesn't notice that I can't hear him, but even if he did, I doubt he'd care. Like most of the stories the young tell the old,

I guess Reza's second tale was never really meant for me anyway. I watch Reza travel down a long metal slide, then imitate a fighter jet as he swoops over to the monkey bars. "How am I doing?" I mutter to my invisible audience. I grit my teeth and slide my hand into my pocket, fingering the note. Maybe now, standing in front of this crowd of children and parents who'd notice if I suddenly disappeared, maybe now is the time to...

"You're doing fine. But you should go over to that bench so that you can keep a clear line of sight on him." Perez's voice crackles over my earpiece. "You've got about fifteen minutes left in your TDE."

"But we just got here. Reza wants to play here longer, and then we—"

"You really should go to the bench now," Perez says in full command voice. "Remember, we can pull you back if we have to." I grudgingly walk to a warm metal bench and lower myself onto it, wiping sweat from my brow.

Reza's finished his story and realizes that the person behind him, who he thought was me, is actually a young father watching his toddler play. Reza's going to panic as he looks for me, so I wave to him. Sure enough, he spots me and runs over.

"Where did you go?" he asks me. "I was telling you a story!"

"You were running too fast," I say. "You'll have to start again."

Reza shakes his head. "No!" he declares. "No starting over. I told the story. It's your fault you didn't listen."

I chuckle quietly. Damn, I used to be precocious. And

stubborn. At least that's stuck with me. "Well, then, how about just the short version?"

"There was a space princess," he says as if that explains it all. Strangely, it does, or at least it explains enough. I remember something about a lizard who took her captive, and she escaped, but the details don't much matter.

"All right," I say. "You owe me one more. Then I'll tell you one."

"What do you want this one to be about?" he asks me. "I don't have an idea for one right now."

"How about someone who does something he isn't supposed to do?" I suggest. The story I've saved for him will give him hope in the days to come. The kid might as well return the favor in advance.

Reza nods assent, but he's distracted by the other kids playing. "Okay. Once upon a time, there was a man who broke the law. He was bad, so they caught him and put him in jail. The end."

"That's not a very good story," I say. "What law did he break?"

Reza sighs and squirms in his suit, turning his attention back to me. "He broke the law that says don't do bad stuff."

"Not helpful," I say. "What bad stuff did he do?"

Reza thinks for a moment. "The man took his sister's phone, but then the man said that he didn't do it, but then his parents found out, and he got in trouble."

"So what did they do with him when they caught him?"

"They put him in a jail that no one can ever escape from."

"Did he try to escape?"

"Yes. He tried every day to escape, but it never worked."

"Never? Why not?"

Reza looks at me like I'm a moron. "Because there are guards with lasers."

"What if he crawled on the ground to escape at night when they couldn't see him?"

"Then he still can't escape because there's an ocean around the whole place."

"But what if he swam across it?"

"Then the alligators in the ocean eat him."

"But what if he beat up the alligators and then swam across?"

"He can't," Reza's word is final. "They're alligators, and he's just normal."

"But he could dig a tunnel and get out."

"No, because he doesn't have a shovel, and even if he gets one, robots would chase him and catch him and bring him back."

I smile sadly at him. "It sounds like you've got everything figured out. There's really no way for this guy to escape."

"Yeah. He just stays there till he dies."

"All because he took his sister's phone?"

Reza nods.

"That seems harsh."

"Well, he shouldn't have took the phone."

My vision goes temporarily wet and blurry. "I don't like that story very much."

Reza shrugs. "Then tell a better one."

I smile. "Okay," I say and stand up, taking Reza's hand.

"I'll try to tell you a better one."

"After the tigers?" Reza's eyes are alight.

My earpiece crackles again, and I hear Perez's voice. "Ten-minute warning." I curse under my breath.

"We don't have time for the tigers," I tell my past self, clearing my throat. "But we do have time for my story before you go."

"I wanna see the tigers!" Reza insists, and for a moment, I worry that he's going to throw a fit, but then I remember that he won't.

"You have to get back to the reception and your parents," I say. "They might be looking for you." Reza pouts all the way back to the path. Meanwhile, I call on every last memory cell to help me conjure what I'm about to say. Finally, I begin. "There's a story that the people of..."

"That's not how stories start," Reza corrects me. "They start 'Once upon a time'."

I shove my hands into my pockets. "It's my story, so I'll start it how I want."

"No, you can't! There are rules," Reza insists. I wonder how many times in the last half hour I've sighed.

"Fine," I relent. I hesitate before continuing, considering telling Reza a very different tale, one about a man full of regrets who's lost everyone he cares about. But what I'm beginning to tell, while ridiculous, will stick with Reza through the years before it fades into his worn, patchy memory. It'll help him get to sleep at night when he worries that what came for his grandpa will come for him. And as I look at the boy, so very small, I realize that I can't be the one who takes that story away from him and leaves him with a tragedy about pain and loss to worry over instead.

"Once upon a time, there was a tribe of people who lived on a small island far away. And they talked about what happens when you die. A lot of other people had different ideas about death. Some people said that when you die, you're taken to a special place far away. Some people said that when you die, that's just it—there's nothing. But the people on this island knew that those things weren't true. When you die, they said, you come back to the world, but you come back as a different person in a different place in a different time. Every single person who ever lived, they said, was really the same person. And every time they died, they forgot everything. And the people on the island refused to fight wars with each other or be mean to each other because they realized that they were all the same person, just at different places and points in time, so if they hurt someone, they'd just be hurting themselves."

"That's not real," Reza says. "We aren't all the same person."

"We could be," I start, and Perez growls a warning "Hilbert" in my ear.

"Maybe," I continue, "you're really the same person as everyone else, the same as your grandpa and your mom and your dad. And every time you die, you get to go back in time and start over as someone else. Like a video game, but you get to play as everyone who's ever lived and who will ever live."

Reza thinks for a second. "So when Grandpa died, he went back in time and became someone new?"

"Yeah," I say. "But he forgot being Grandpa."

"I think I like that," Reza says. "It makes dying not scary. All the stories Mom and Dad and everyone at the funeral told about dying are scary, but that one's not scary."

"I like it too," I say. "But even if you don't like that story, there's no reason to be scared of death. It's better to only be scared about the things you have control over."

"Like snakes," Reza says gravely, and I remember the constrictor I saw in a nature documentary when I was six, and how terrible those coiled muscles all bunched in a pile had looked.

"Yes," I say. "Like snakes."

Suddenly we're on the steps in front of the church again, and it makes no sense to me because it feels like we just left the park a moment ago. Perez's voice crackles over my earpiece with my one-minute warning, and I'm frantically trying to remember when I missed her five-minute warning. As I realize where I am and how close my TDE is to ending, my pulse races, and my stomach clenches.

It can't end now. I just need a little more time.

"Reza," I say, turning quickly to him, and I think Perez may be saying something over the earpiece, but I have no time left for my fear to trick me into wasting. "There are things I need to tell you—" Abruptly, I feel the harness warming up, its purr growing louder. Our time is up, and somehow, I got too scattered, too afraid of missing my chance, too caught up in little Reza's world to do what I needed to do.

I clutch at the note in my pocket, and one last desperate ray of hope cuts through the fog in my brain. As Reza turns to sit back down on the top step, I pull out my note and stuff it into the back pocket of Reza's pants. He may not be able to make any sense of my scribbles, but maybe a word or two will stick. Maybe it will be enough to change things. It has to be better than nothing. After what I've given him, it's the least he can do for me.

As I step back from him, Reza looks up at me.

"Thanks for taking me to the park," he says with the mechanical politeness his father drilled into him. "And I liked your story."

"I liked your stories too," I say, smiling at him as tears well up in my eyes once more. "Live a good life, Reza, and make better choices than I did."

"Aren't you going inside?" Reza asks, and I know he doesn't understand what I've just told him to do, but I'm moving as quickly as I can through the parking lot and to the privacy of the wooded path.

"I can't," I shout back. "Please just tell them that I love them all and that you love them, and..." But I'm out of earshot and into the trees. My harness roars, and I collapse in a sweaty, convulsing heap. Then the world comes back into focus, and with it, a kind of lightness. I've done all I can do. The note will have to be enough.

* * *

The trip back to the USTTD building and my subsequent evaluations pass as a blur. I don't give the techs even half of my attention as I force myself from memory to memory, searching for any indication that I received and read that note as a child. But I can't remember finding or reading any note from myself, and my memories of Nadia's death and Amy's are clear as ever.

"Maybe time travel interacts with memories strangely," I think. "Time paradoxes create all sorts of strange effects in movies. Maybe I'll go home and discover Brianna and Amy waiting for me. Maybe I'll get a letter or text from Nadia."

Perez clears her throat to pull me back into the present, and I'm not sure how long she's been standing there. "We're nearly done here, Mr. Hilbert," she says. "Just one last detail." She nods to the techs to let them know they can leave, and we're suddenly alone in her office.

I feel a lump in my throat but put on a smile. "What's that?"

"This." Perez draws a crumpled yellow note—my crumpled yellow note—from her pocket and tosses it on the desk in front of me.

My mouth tastes like ash. "Where did you—"

"Church steps," she replies, shaking her head. "After your TDE. That note was in your pocket when you entered the ionization chamber?"

"How... why is it *here*?"

"Anything you carried into the ionization chamber was keyed to your harness, just like your clothes. The note was still in the harness's transit radius when we pulled you back, so it came with you."

I lean back in my chair, eyes floating to the off-white ceiling. "I should've thought of that."

"So you knowingly violated our directives and tried to leave a future artifact with your past self?"

I throw up my hands. "Yeah, I left the note to change the past. I violated your rules. Go ahead and arrest me."

"What did it say?" Perez asks, and I'm confused.

"Didn't you read it?"

"It was illegible. The ink was smeared."

I look at my hand and see trails of black ink etched in its cracks, staining my sweat.

"So what did it say?"

My heart sinks down, down, down. "Nothing. Just... nothing important." My plan, my actions, were futile, frustrated in a myriad of ways, some of which I would probably never even know about.

"Then why did you give it to him?"

"You know my history," I tell her. "After the loss of every person I've ever cared about, why wouldn't I risk prison for the chance to have my daughter back or my sister back or to actually make something of myself?"

Perez is silent for a moment. "I get it. It was a deeply stupid thing to do, but I get it."

I lean back, resigning myself. "So are you going to arrest me?"

"No."

"No?" I take a ragged breath. "So... you're going to do something worse, then?"

She exhales a clipped laugh. "You watch too much television. Your TDE was a success; the TAA was resolved, and here you sit looking no worse than you did before we sent you half a century into the past. The government is happy. The universe is happy. Just stick to the agreements you signed from here on out, and I'll be happy."

"No!" I shout, slamming my fist on her desk and rising

from the chair as fast as my still-recovering legs let me. "You can't just ignore what I did, just act like what I did didn't count! I broke your rules, and actions have to have consequences, and I..." I trail off as my body starts to shake, and my eyes brim with tears.

Perez raises her eyebrows, and for a moment, I think I see something resembling human pity in those brown pits. "And you don't think your TDE had any consequences?"

"Nothing's changed. Amy and Nadia are still dead. Nothing that happened in that TDE mattered, not really, which means that whole trip, all of it, was for nothing."

Perez looks at me like I'm still six. "Hilbert, I've spent most of my professional life thinking about time, so believe me when I say you're thinking about this the wrong way. It's like you said during your TDE: it's better to only be scared of the things you have control over. You're so hung up on your inability to change the past that you're ignoring the fact that, in a sense, you *succeeded* in changing the past."

"What?"

"You told little Reza that story. You acted autonomously and authentically, and you gave a little boy hope. No, your potentially suicidal plan didn't work out as you hoped. But that doesn't change the importance of what you succeeded in doing."

I shake my head. "But that's not a change! I remember being told that story. It had to happen."

"It only had to happen because you chose to make it happen. If you had chosen differently, you would have remembered it differently. This past event may have been fixed, but it was your actions, your choice that fixed it."

It's not the first time Perez has made this point, but for some reason, standing in her office with sweat pouring down my face, eyes watery, and hands shaking, her words finally penetrate my thick skull. It's a moment of ecstasy and of panic. For just a moment, I see an ocean of eternity filled with immutably fixed points, Amy's death and Nadia's, Brianna and my ink-stained palms, and my story to little Reza. But I am the wave that connects all of these points, and that makes my story to Reza, sitting right on my crest, both perfectly free and perfectly predetermined. The contradiction exhausts me, and as the wave crashes, my spinning head dumps me back into Perez's office unceremoniously.

Perez's expression verges on genuine concern. "You okay, Hilbert?"

I nod and smile, then make my way toward the door. "Yeah, I'm good. I think I'm starting to get this time stuff. Not, you know, fully, but kind of. Focus on the things you have control over and all that."

She smiles and leans back in her chair. "Sounds about right. Now go live the rest of your life."

I walk out the door and into the hallway. I feel the rough edges of the wadded-up note in my hand. There's a garbage can to my left, right next to the exit. I walk to it and place the note in my back pocket.

Then I pull out my pack of cigarettes and toss them in the trash.

* * *

This story is a part of our legacy-of-excellence program, first printed in the After Dinner Conversation—December 2020 issue.

Discussion Questions

1. According to Perez (*the scientist*), regardless of what you do, the past cannot be changed. This means whatever did happen will happen. Lincoln will die. Assuming this is true, does this mean there is no free will or real choice?
2. Do you personally believe you have free will? How could you prove your answer one way or the other?
3. What key things do you think the narrator is trying to change with the items written on his list? If you could slip your younger self a piece of paper with just a few words written on it, would you? If so, what would be the things you would want to change, and why those things?
4. What are you saying about your current self, and about your past choices, when you attempt to provide information to your younger self, so you would make different choices?
5. According to the narrator's story, we are all just one person "at different places and points in time." What do you think of this idea? Is there a story you would want to go back and tell your child self? If so, what story, and for what reason?

* * *

Boomchee

Shani Naylor

***

I saw Barry this morning in Pak'nSave. A tall, older man with thick gray hair pushing a supermarket trolley. Even though I hadn't seen him for about twenty-five years, he was unmistakable. I didn't call out or wave. He wouldn't know me from the crowd of middle-aged women doing their weekly shopping. He made me think of Susie.

It was her bright smile that first drew my attention to Susie. I'd been working at the Glaxo factory for a week and was still trying to put names to faces. I was one of a group of six university students who had answered an ad for a summer job back in the day when Glaxo had its big pharmaceutical factory in Palmerston North.

The students were given a range of jobs in the factory. Some were fun, like working the huge guillotine that cut through heavy stacks of cardboard or the machine that wrapped boxes in sheets of plastic and sealed the edges with heat. But some jobs were straight-out boring, like working on the conveyor belt. This involved taking things off the conveyor belt and putting them into boxes. I can't even remember what we took off the conveyor belt. Little tubes of... something? When the students worked on the conveyor belt, we used to chat and laugh and tell jokes to pass the time of day. But I noticed that some of the permanent staff really had to focus to do the job. They found our chitchat and laughter distracting. I wondered what they really thought of us, this group of smart people who came in and picked up their jobs for a couple of months to make a few bucks and then took off back to university. Maybe they resented us.

But Susie wasn't like that. She was the sweetest thing. And really quite pretty. She had curly blonde hair and was rather curvaceous (although a nasty person might call her plump). She had such a sunny nature, always saying hello and laughing at our jokes (even when I suspected she didn't really understand them) with a big smile on her face. I knew my boyfriend, Martin, would say Susie wasn't the sharpest tool in the shed, but that didn't matter. She was like the kid in your class at school who always got the lowest score but was happy anyway. I felt a bit sorry for her. This was probably the best job she could hope to get. When I qualified as a lawyer and was doing amazing things in court, she'd still be here, sitting by the conveyor belt, picking things up and putting them into boxes. I don't think she could even work the guillotine or the plastic wrapping machine. I chatted with her one day when we were sitting next to each other. I found out she was twenty-six, lived at home with her parents, had a cat called Wendy, and had never had a boyfriend (she got a bit shy when I asked her about that). She was a lovely girl.

That summer was the longest holiday Martin and I spent together. We'd hooked up near the end of the previous summer when we'd met at a music festival. We sort of knew each other from school anyway. Then he went to Otago to do pre-med, and I went to Vic to do law. We kept in touch during term time and spent our holidays back home in Palmy.

That was where I met Martin's older brother Barry, who still lived at home with their mother, even though he was in his mid-thirties. Martin also had two older sisters, but they had moved away, married, and had families. Martin was the baby, born when his mother was forty-five.

Martin's mum fussed over Barry. She did all the housework and got up early every morning to cook him breakfast, even though she had quite bad arthritis. Barry helped around the garden, mowed the lawn, and drove his mother if she needed to go anywhere.

Martin complained constantly about his brother. "Bloody Barry, he's got Mum twisted around his little finger. He should make his own frickin' breakfast."

I would say: "Well, at least she's got someone at home to keep an eye on her." I didn't say: "She makes your breakfast too, Martin, when you're home."

Barry was a bit odd. It was difficult to put your finger on exactly why. He was always very formal, even with Martin. He worked in the kind of old-fashioned men's clothing shop that sold cardigans and slacks. Apart from work, he stayed home, watched television, did stuff around the house, and that was about it. He wasn't unpleasant or anything. He was always polite and said hello, but apart from that never took any interest in me. I thought maybe that was because I was at university, and he felt intimidated. In hindsight, I think it was probably because I just didn't matter to him. These days, people would say he was on the spectrum. I thought he was just a bit different. He wasn't bad looking, though—being tall with nice thick brown hair.

One day when I'd been working at the Glaxo factory for a couple of weeks, I had a brilliant idea. How about setting up Barry and Susie on a blind date? They were both single, both nice people, and both unlikely to meet someone without a helping hand. I told Martin my idea, and he was horrified.

"No bloody way! It's a terrible idea."

"But why not?"

"We can't just interfere in their lives."

"It's not interfering—we can ask them, and if they're not interested, then that's the end of it."

Martin wasn't convinced. I pleaded. I told him about Susie and how sweet she was. I said it would be good for Barry to interact with a woman who wasn't his mother. It took a week, but I wore him down. In the end, Martin agreed, probably just to shut me up.

We talked about how it might work, and, in the end, we agreed that we couldn't just set up a blind date and leave them to it. Neither of them, to our knowledge, had been out with someone of the opposite sex before, so it would be doomed to failure. We would have to go with them and guide them in the right direction.

Martin was still reluctant, but I convinced him I had a

good plan. I think he was worried I'd suggest going somewhere like the Fitz or the Fat Ladies Arms, where he'd be bound to run into his mates. Instead, I suggested the Awapuni Hotel.

"It's perfect," I said. "They have a buffet and a covers band. Do you know anyone who's ever gone there?"

He couldn't think of one person.

"Then we won't see anyone we know. Barry and Susie can have a meal and then dance. We'll keep everything on track, and if they want to see each other again, they can use the phone like everyone else."

At that point, Martin seemed to run out of excuses, so he agreed.

"Perfect. You talk to Barry, and I'll talk to Susie," I said.

Susie was easy. At morning tea the next day, I mentioned that my boyfriend had a brother who was single, and perhaps she'd like to meet him. I didn't need to convince her. She said yes straight away. And she looked so excited. She was almost jumping up and down when she returned to the conveyor belt. After that, at every opportunity, she came over to talk to me and ask questions. What should she wear? What was Barry like? Did he have a job? What sort of dancing were they going to do? She told some of her friends at the factory, and they got all excited as well. Honestly, they were like a bunch of schoolgirls. Some of the students found out as well. A couple of them seemed to think it was a joke. One asked me: "Are you sure you know what you're doing?"

Barry turned out to be easy as well. I had half thought he would refuse, but, to Martin's surprise, he agreed immediately. Well, that was good, then.

On Saturday night, I went around to Susie's house to pick her up. She looked lovely. She was wearing a pale blue dress with a lacy white collar and cuffs that she'd worn to a cousin's wedding. To be honest, she looked a bit over-dressed for Palmy on a Saturday night, but I didn't want to suggest that she change. Susie's father looked at her proudly, but her mother pulled me aside and asked me to keep an eye on her.

"Of course, I will."

"She's not like you university girls."

"I know. I promise I'll look after Susie."

She looked me up and down. Finally, "Okay then. Off you go."

We drove to the Awapuni Hotel and arrived just as Martin and Barry were getting out of their car. Barry was wearing a suit with a tie and looked a bit flustered. I did the introductions, and Barry put out his hand to shake Susie's. Then Barry and Martin walked in, and Susie and I followed. I caught her eye and winked, and she giggled loudly.

There were a handful of families with children and some older couples in the restaurant. Martin and I did most of the talking and ended up asking questions to get the conversation going. We found out what school Susie had gone to, where her grandparents lived, where she liked going for holidays, and how long she had worked at Glaxo (nine years!). Barry talked about his favorite television shows and told us what he sold in the shop (four types of cardigans, I knew it!). At one point, Martin and I locked eyes. I could see he was thinking the same as me, that everything was going great.

The band started playing after dinner. They were

actually quite good. They started off with real oldies from the fifties and earlier. To get things going, I asked Barry to dance, and then Martin asked Susie. Some of the older people were doing the proper ballroom stuff, and we tried to follow suit. It was fun. Even stiff old Barry seemed to be getting into it. Then we swapped partners, and I danced with Martin while Barry danced with Susie. By this point, the band was playing more modern songs, so Martin and I did our usual boogying, but Barry and Susie kept dancing together with his arms around her. What a cute couple! They looked like they were really enjoying it. Martin had been so negative, yet Barry and Susie were having a great time. It was a triumph!

At the end of the night, I was to take Susie home. She and Barry said their goodbyes in the car park—Susie's face was pink and flushed from dancing. I don't know how Barry could resist kissing her goodnight. Maybe he felt shy with his brother and me standing there.

Susie was very animated on the drive home. She'd had a wonderful time and couldn't stop talking about it. She kept thanking me for introducing her to Barry and saying how nice he was. Her parents looked relieved to see her. Her father shook my hand, and her mother kissed me on the cheek. She had a tear in her eye.

Then I drove back to Martin's place. Barry and his mother were sitting at the dining table drinking cocoa, and Martin was slouched on the sofa watching TV. I sat at the table and looked at Barry. He seemed pleased in his usual reserved way.

"Did you enjoy your night?" I asked.

"Yes, it was very pleasant, thank you."

"And Susie?"

"She was very nice."

"And... would you like to see her again?"

"I don't think that's a good idea," said Barry. "Because of Boomchee."

"Boom... sorry?"

"Boomchee. My fiancée."

"What the hell?" Martin jumped up from the sofa. "Did you say fiancée?" He looked from Barry to his mother.

"Yes, my fiancée. She's coming to live here in March."

"Did you know about this, Mum?" Martin was almost shouting.

"Yes, of course. I've spoken to Boomchee a few times on the phone. She's a lovely girl. Her English isn't so good, but it'll improve."

"Where's she from?" I asked.

"Thailand," said Barry.

"Why didn't someone tell me?" said Martin.

"Barry wanted to keep it private," Martin's mother said. "Besides, it was only confirmed a few days ago. Boomchee will come here to live, and, all going well, she and Barry will get married mid-year."

"But have you even met her?" Martin asked Barry. "You haven't, have you? You don't even know what she looks like."

"Yes, I do," said Barry. "I've got a photo." He stood up and left the room.

"She's only after his money," said Martin. "He knows that, right?"

"Well, he's hardly John-Paul Getty, is he?" said his mother. "Boomchee is a hard worker and very respectful of her elders. She'll be a great help around the house."

"I can't believe what I'm hearing," said Martin.

Barry came back with a black and white passport-type photo showing a serious-looking young Asian woman with long hair pulled back into a ponytail.

"She looks nice," I said.

Martin glanced at it and turned away. "So, why did you come out tonight if you already have a fiancée?"

Barry looked uncomfortable. "I've never been out with a lady before. I thought it would be good practice for when Boomchee arrives."

"For fuck's sake," said Martin. He looked at me. "Let's go to your place."

Martin was silent during the fifteen-minute drive to my house. His knuckles were white as he gripped the steering wheel.

I had a thought. "She might be a prostitute," I said.

"Give it a rest," he hissed, as though I'd been banging on about Boomchee all night.

* * *

On Monday at work, I didn't know what to say to Susie. I couldn't tell her about Boomchee. I couldn't say that Barry had a fiancée all along that he hadn't told us about. Poor, sweet, trusting Susie. She wouldn't understand. She'd think I had done it on purpose. I saw her in the staff room, putting on a white coat before she saw me. She had the same bouncy look and big smile that she'd had when I dropped her at home on Saturday night. I couldn't face her.

I put on my white coat and swept past. "Hi, Susie. Hope you enjoyed Saturday night." Then I strode over to the guillotine and didn't look back. At morning tea, I took the last seat next to the other students and talked loudly to them. At lunchtime, I snuck out and went to the local shops for half an hour. I kept this up every day. One tea break, I even hid in the loo for ten minutes. Every time Susie came near, I would say hello, then take myself somewhere else. By mid-week, she had got the message. At that point, I could see she wasn't her usual bubbly self. I felt really bad. I knew it was cowardly of me. I should have said something, but I just didn't know what to do. A couple of the students asked me about the blind date. I said it was fine, and they left it at that. Some of the permanent staff must have heard something because they gave me rather nasty looks. But they didn't say anything.

That was the last week of the summer holidays before we went back to uni. I phoned in sick for work on my last day, so I didn't have to speak to anyone. Martin was still angry. His mother and brother should have told him about Boomchee earlier.

Martin was really busy that year. Medicine was a huge commitment, and he didn't have much time for anything else. When the next holidays rolled around, I went to Tauranga with some flatmates instead of going to see my folks in Palmy. After a couple of months, Martin and I were officially over. I wasn't bothered. I had met a guy in Tauranga and dropped out of uni to be with him. Law was too much work anyway. I got a job in a café. It didn't last. The job or the guy.

I heard through the Palmy grapevine that Barry had gotten married to a Thai woman. I never knew what had happened to Susie. Did she meet someone else? Did she work at Glaxo's until she was made redundant when the factory closed?

Even now, decades later, I still wonder about Susie and feel bad about what happened.

When I got made redundant, I came back to live in my parents' old house in Palmy. A couple of months later, I saw Barry picking feijoas in the fruit section at Pak'nSave. I saw him again in the car park with two people—a middle-aged Asian woman and a teenage girl who looked like a younger, taller version of the woman. They were loading groceries into a car. The girl said something, and the adults laughed. They looked happy together.

I put my groceries into my car: one chop, a few spuds, two-minute noodles, bananas, and baked beans. I thought how nice it would be to have someone to laugh with. I'm glad Barry found Boomchee.

* * *

This story is a part of our legacy-of-excellence program, first printed in the After Dinner Conversation—January 2021 issue.

Discussion Questions

1. What is your opinion of Barry marrying Boomchee?
2. Do you think it was wrong for Barry, who was engaged, to go out with Susie? What, if anything, should he have done differently?
3. Barry and Boomchee ended up happily married with a teenager. The narrator ended up alone *(but wishing she had married someone)*. Do the outcomes change your opinion of Barry's choice to get a "mail-order bride?"
4. Is falling in love (1) an emotion, (2) a choice, or (3) a combination of the two? How is it that arranged marriages *(or mail-order brides)* have success *(or love?)* when so many dates don't work out? *(The divorce rate for arranged marriages is 4 percent versus 40 percent in the US)*
5. What, if any, mistakes did Barry, Susie, the narrator, or anyone else make in the story?

* * *

Author Information

Thorn

Erik Fatemi lives in Arlington, Virginia. A former newspaper editor and columnist, he now lobbies the federal government on behalf of nonprofit health groups. His fiction has also been published in *JMWW*, *Identity Theory*, and *WWPH Writes*. Twitter @ErikFatemi.

What We Talk About When We Talk About Reincarnation

Edward Daschle *(he/him/his)* is a student of fiction in the University of Maryland's creative writing MFA program. He grew up in the Pacific Northwest, land of serial killers and Sasquatch, deadly mountains and overcast skies. His fiction also appears in *Grim & Gilded*, *Stoneboat Literary Journal*, *Defunct*, and *OFIC Magazine*.

The House Of God

Shannon Frost Greenstein (she/her) resides in Philadelphia with her children and soulmate. She is the author of "These Are a Few of My Least Favorite Things," a full-length book of poetry available from Really Serious Literature, and "Pray for Us Sinners," a short story collection with Alien Buddha Press. Shannon is a former Ph.D. candidate in Continental Philosophy and a multi-time Pushcart Prize nominee. Her work has appeared in McSweeney's Internet Tendency, Pithead Chapel, Bending Genres, and elsewhere. www.shannonfrostgreenstein.com; Twitter @ShannonFrostGre

Visions Of Midwives

C.S. Griffel teaches English and Creative Writing at a small university in central Texas. Besides short stories, she writes screenplays and is learning to love poetry. Her stories also appear in the *William and Mary Review* and *Talon Review*. She is also published in "I Found Happiness and Tragedy: Selections from the 2022 Literary Taxidermy Competition."

Playing God

Ilan Herman is a professional freelance writer and a published fiction and nonfiction author. He lives in northern CA and is available for all your writing and editing needs. *www.righteous-writing.com*

And Joy Shall Overtake Us As A Flood

Daniel James Peterson is a philosopher, writer, and non-profit executive director living in Decatur, Georgia. He teaches philosophy at Morehouse College and has published academic papers on a variety of topics including the philosophy of physics and the philosophy of education. His fiction has appeared in the magazines *Analog*, *Anotherrealm*, and *Every Day Fiction*.
www.danieljamespeterson.com

Boomchee

Shani Naylor lives in Wellington, New Zealand, and is a former journalist. She has had short fiction published in the Top of the Morning Book of Incredibly Short Stories, *Flash Frontier*, *Toasted Cheese*, *The Drabble*, *Punt Volat* and the *Fairlight Books* site, and selected for broadcast on Scotland's Heartland FM. In 2020 she was longlisted for the Michael Gifkins unpublished novel contest. She is working on an historic novella. Twitter @ShaninNZ

Additional Information

Reviews

If you enjoyed reading these stories, please consider doing an online review. It's only a few seconds of your time, but it is very important in continuing the series. Good reviews mean higher rankings. Higher rankings mean more sales and a greater ability to release stories.

Print Anthology Series

https://www.afterdinnerconversation.com

Purchase our growing collection of print anthologies. They are collections of our best short stories published in the After Dinner Conversation series, complete with discussion questions.

Podcast Discussions/Audiobooks

https://www.afterdinnerconversation.com/podcastlinks

Listen to our podcast discussions and audiobooks of After Dinner Conversation short stories on Apple, Spotify, or wherever podcasts are played. Or, if you prefer, watch the podcasts on our YouTube channel or download the .mp3 file directly from our website.

Patreon

https://www.patreon.com/afterdinnerconversation

Get early access to short stories and ad-free podcasts. New supporters also get a free digital copy of the anthology *After Dinner Conversation–Season One*. Support us on Patreon!

Book Clubs/Classrooms

https://www.afterdinnerconversation.com/book-club-downloads

After Dinner Conversation supports book clubs! Receive free short stories for your book club to read and discuss!

Social

Connect with us on Facebook, YouTube, Instagram, TikTok, and Twitter.

Made in the USA
Middletown, DE
29 March 2023

27171696R00073